GAMBLER'S
GOLD

CALIBER
BOOKS

Also from DOYLE TRENT

GAMBLER'S GOLD: Tales of the Old Wild West
Book Two

For further information visit the Caliber Comics website:
www.calibercomics.com

Cover image by: Dubya2x

CHAPTER 1

J.B. Watts had suffered through just about all the bad luck a man could stand in one week. That's what he thought at the time. He was wrong.

"There wasn't one chance in a thousand of that feller drawin' four aces," he said to the blue-roan gelding he was riding. "Not one chance in a million."

The horse cocked one ear back at him and went on climbing a steep wagon trail north of Santa Fe. J.B. sat the low-fork, rim-fire saddle lazily. He had wrapped the reins once around the saddle horn and passed the ends under his left thigh to hold them while he rolled a Bull Durham cigarette. He was talking to the horse—and to himself.

"Wouldn't you know it. The only time in my life I ever drew kings full and somebody draws four aces. There wasn't one chance in a thousand of losin' that hand. But ol' hard-luck J.B. Watts could lose. Hell, I can lose anytime anyplace. If I had four aces, somebody'd have a straight flush."

He struck a wooden match on the rock-hard rawhide wrapped around the saddle horn, cupped the match between both hands, and lit the cigarette. He shook the match, pinched it between two fingers and snapped it in two before dropping it.

"I did one thing right. I quit before I was put afoot. With my luck, if I'd cut the cards with that feller for my horse and outfit like he wanted to, I prob'ly wouldn't have nothin' left.

"I still got you, Ol' Amigo. Ugly as you are, I wouldn't trade you for a Kentucky thoroughbred." The horse, a long-backed, long-necked animal, picked its way over the rocks where they had taken a shortcut across a curve in the road. J.B. went on grumbling.

Two months' wages wiped out. Two months of riding circle, gathering cows and calves, rasslin' calves and holding them down while they were branded, castrated, and earmarked. Two months of sleeping on the ground, eating beans, biscuits, and tough beef. He should have stayed on at the Diamond A, he mused. At least he'd know where his next meal was coming from.

But no, his drifting ways couldn't be changed. Not even when the foreman had offered him a steady job.

"You ain't very big, but you're not lazy and you're not stupid," the foreman had said. "The days of the free range're comin' to an end and we're gonna go to fencin' around here. We can always use another good, steady hand. Hell, son, you gotta stay in one place, get some roots down if you're gonna amount to anything."

But no. He didn't like to even think about fences and he wasn't about to dig portholes. His hands were made for reins and a rope, not a posthole digger. And besides, he was a born drifter, too curious about what was over the horizon to stay in one place very long.

For the first day or two after he had drawn his wages and had ridden into Santa Fe, he was content to sit in the plaza and watch the people go by. Especially the pretty senoritas. Watching people was something he always enjoyed after being out in the hills for months. But eventually he got bored and, having nothing else to do, started gambling. There were plenty of opportunities to gamble. The cowtowns and trade towns were full of sharpsters waiting for someone like J.B. Watts to come along, someone with several months' wages in his pocket.

They let him win at first. That made it easier to entice others into the game. Then, after three days, they decided to clean him out. He was so broke when he left the game he couldn't pay the bill at the second-rate hotel where he had been staying, and he left without picking up his belongings. The hotel manager would sell them, he knew, and keep the money.

"If a rattlesnake had my brain, it'd crawl backwards," J.B. said to the horse. "I wish I could say easy come easy go, but hell, it didn't come so easy."

He pushed back the curl-brim, black hat and wiped a shirt sleeve across his forehead. A shock of reddish-blond hair fell across his face. He squinted at the sky with pale blue eyes and allowed as how it was going to rain.

J.B. Watts was a small, slender young man. His complexion, which went with the light-colored hair, was the easily sun-reddened kind, and his short nose was always peeling. He was no toughy, but had a straight mouth and square chin which told the world he was no softy either. He wore a khaki shirt and Levi's with the legs tucked into the tops of high-heeled riding boots.

He was heading for El Rey, where, he had been told, the Diamond A Land and Cattle Company had another, larger cow outfit. It took all summer and half the winter to gather and brand the calves at El Rey, they said, and maybe he could get a job.

If he didn't starve first. Or drown.

"It's sure as hell gonna rain," he said to the gelding. "Cowmen've been bellyachin' for rain and there wasn't a cloud in the sky—'till I lost my slicker. Now it's gonna rain like a cow unloadin' on a rock. And I'll bet there ain't a roof anywhere this side of El Rey."

He was right. Jagged lightning streaked across the sky, thunder boomed and cracked. A fat drop of rain fell on his left shoulder, then another. He topped a small rise, reined his horse to a stop, stood in his stirrups and looked ahead. The country was dotted with piñon pines and scarred with rocky ravines.

Off to the east of the wagon road was a deep ravine with a shallow end. He turned the blue-roan toward it. "Let's git down there where we ain't so good a target for that lightnin'," he said. Cold, high-country rain began falling steadily. "Let's lope, Ol' Amigo."

Once in the ravine, J.B. followed a dry streambed for a short distance and discovered a rock overhang made by water perhaps a thousand years before. He dismounted and untied the bed tarp he had rolled up behind the cantle board. It and a change of socks were all he owned now besides the horse and saddle.

He draped the long canvas over his head and crawled on his hands and knees under the overhang. "Your hide sheds water better than mine does, Ol' Amigo," he said by way of apology to the horse.

J.B. huddled there, watching his saddle get thoroughly wet and thinking about how cold the leather was going to be when he got back into it. He thought about his empty stomach and wondered how he could wrangle a meal when he got to El Rey.

He shivered and wished the sky would clear and the sun would come out and warm things up again. The blue-roan put its head down, humped its back, and stood there, waiting patiently.

"I should've gone into farmin' with my brothers," he grumbled, "Hell, they'll work their butts to a frazzle tryin' to get a cotton crop off of eighty acres of sand, but they've got chickens and hogs and they'll never go hungry. They sure as hell ain't settin' out here in the cold and the rain with their belly buttons knockin' on their backbones."

J.B. couldn't help it. He was feeling sorry for himself. He was sorry for the way he was brought up—on a South Texas dry-dirt farm with two older brothers who were always picking on him because he was the smallest—for having to quit school after only four years, and for the death of his parents, who had worked their hearts out trying to make a living at small-scale cotton farming. Thinking back, J.B. remembered that he had always wanted to be a cowboy since the first time he saw a crew of cowboys working cattle in the mesquites just north of his folks' farm. At thirteen he had talked himself into a job with that crew. He was a hard worker, and one day the foreman told him the fall beef roundup was about to start and if he'd get himself a saddle and outfit he could go along. That was fourteen years ago, and he'd been a cowboy ever since.

It was a hard life, with few rewards. The wages he got always seemed to leak from his pockets. If a girl didn't get his money, the gamblers did. He was always a loser.

"Damn," he said, pulling the tarp farther over his head and leaning back against the rock wall. "One of these damn days I'm gonna git smart and find an easier way to make money. Yessir, there's

8

got to be an easier way."

He was sitting there, thinking thoughts like that, when he found the gold.

He had put his hand out to support himself while he shifted positions, and he felt something soft and slippery. The next thought that came into his mind was RATTLESNAKE, and he jumped as if he had been kicked in the seat. He grabbed a rock to throw at the snake, and looked back to see where it was.

What he saw surprised and puzzled him at the same time.

It was a tightly rolled bundle, wrapped in yellow oilskin and tied with leather thongs. It looked like a rain slicker rolled up to tie behind a saddle.

"Now what in the humped-up world is that doin' here?" J.B. asked himself. He pulled it out of a wide crack in the rocks and tried to untie the thongs. They were damp and impossible to loosen. He dug a folding knife out of his pants pocket, cut the thongs, and unrolled the package.

It was a rain slicker, all right, a well-used one, frayed at the collar and cuffs. A large "CC" was painted in white on the front.

"Maybe my luck has changed," J.B. said. "There ain't one chance in a thousand of a wet cowboy settin' under a rock and findin' a rain slicker bundled up and layin' beside 'im."

He stood up, shucked the bed tarp, and put on the slicker. The left side contained a pocket, and the pocket was heavy. J.B. reached in and pulled out a leather pouch about three times the size of a tobacco sack and tied with another leather thong.

He untied it, looked inside, and was stunned.

The cowboy scrambled away from the overhanging rock and looked around. He looked up both ends of the ravine, climbed up on top and looked. The only living creature he saw was his horse.

"Good gawd amighty," he whispered, as if he feared he would be heard. He slid on the seat of the slicker back down into the ravine and stood for a moment before the overhang. He got down onto his hands and knees and poked around under the overhang, searching every crack, wondering if he would find anything else. He found nothing.

He stood up and looked carefully again up and down the ravine.

He opened the pouch again and poured the gold coins out into his hand. There were about twenty of them, all double eagles. He knew they were worth more than a cowboy would earn in a year.

For a long while, J.B. Watts stood there, staring at the gold coins in his hand. He looked at the horse. The horse dozed, a good indication that no living creature bigger than an ant was anywhere near. The rain poured down. His hat and the slicker were keeping J.B. dry down to his ankles, but his feet were wet. He wasn't aware that his feet were wet. "Good gawd amighty," he whispered again. Finally, he poured the coins back into the pouch and tied it. Moving slowly, as if in a trance, he rolled up the bed tarp and tied it behind his saddle with the ends hanging down on each side. He picked up the reins, tightened the cinch, and stepped into the saddle. The blue-roan moved out lively, happy to be traveling again.

J.B. rode out the shallow end of the ravine, stopped, took another long look around, and rode on.

The blue-roan's comfortable, long-legged running walk covered two or three miles before the cowboy spoke again. J.B. had been doing some serious thinking. "They cain't be real," he said aloud. "Nobody is gonna leave a sack of double eagles and a slicker under a rock like that. They cain't be real."

He rode silently another mile, then, "Unless they was left there for somebody to pick up. Yeah, that's gotta be it. Somebody left 'em there for somebody to pick up. There wasn't one chance in a thousand that a stranger would come along and find 'em." He rode another mile. "Now what in hell am I gonna do with 'em? Somebody's gonna be madder'n a crow on a wet nest when he finds this money gone."

He lifted the reins and brought the horse to a standstill. "I oughta take 'em back. Lord knows I could use some coins, but a feller can get in a hell of a jackpot talkn' somethin' that don't belong to 'im.

"But how do I know they wasn't lost? Could've fell off somebody's saddle and rolled under them rocks. No, they couldn't of got hid between the rocks by accident. No, they was put there a-purpose.

"Good gawd amighty. What do you think I oughta do, Ol' Amigo?"

The horse gave him something else to think about.

Its head came up higher and it looked off to the north. Riders were coming, and they were coming at a gallop.

There were four of them, all wearing yellow slickers. J.B. kept his horse still and waited. They rode up fast, the horses' hooves rattling over the rocks. It didn't matter, but J.B. noticed out of habit that the horses were shod, indicating that the men were not a cowboy crew riding remuda horses.

They were polite at first. "Howdy," said a lean jawed middle-aged rider. He squinted at J.B., his eyes serious under bushy black eyebrows.

"Howdy," J.B. said.

"Which way did you come from?" the lean-jawed man asked. "Santa Fe?"

"Yeah."

"See anybody?"

"Ain't seen nobody all day."

"Well, we're lookin' for—" The rider suddenly stopped talking and stared at the slicker J.B. was wearing. He unbuttoned his own slicker.

The first thing J.B. noticed was the sheriff's star pinned to the man's shirt under the slicker, and the next thing he noticed was the bore of the six-gun.

"Get down," the lawman ordered. "And keep your hands in plain sight."

J.B. kept his seat, puzzled. T\ro more of the riders brought six-guns from under their slickers. The rain hammered down.

"Get off that horse, young feller, before I shoot you off, and do it right now." The pistol was aimed at J.B.'s chest and it didn't waver.

Stiffly, and still puzzled, J.B. dismounted.

"Shuck that raincoat."

J.B. unbuttoned the coat and let it slide from his shoulders and arms to the ground.

The four riders dismounted, and one of them picked up the slicker. He immediately found the pouch and the gold coins. He held it up for the others to see.

The man with the badge stepped closer, his gun aimed steadily at J.B.'s middle. "What'd you do with the body?"

"Wha...what?" J.B. gulped, his eyes fixed on the gun. "What body?"

"Len Crandall's body. You know what I'm talkin' about."

"I didn't see no body."

The man holding the pouch spoke up in a mocking tone. "Oh, he didn't see no body." J.B. glanced at the man. He was big, about an ax handle and a half across the shoulders, J.B. estimated, with a short neck and a thick-jawed face. "I suppose he just found Len's slicker and money poke," the man went on.

"Yeah, yes, yessir," J.B. stammered. "I found 'em in a 'royo back there."

"Sure, sure," the big man mocked. "You just happened to be riding down arroyos and you struck it rich."

J.B. tried to think of something to say, but he couldn't.

"He ain't packin' iron," another rider put in.

The sheriff looked J.B. over, from his boots to his hat, then studied the blue-roan, the saddle, and the bed tarp tied behind the saddle. "You got a gun, young feller? In your boots, or maybe rolled up in that tarp?"

"No. Nossir. I don't own a gun."

The big man untied the tarp and shook it out. All that fell out was a pair of socks.

"You're travelin' light, ain't you, young feller?" the lawman said.

"Yessir."

"Take off them boots."

"What? Why?"

"There's guns little enough to fit inside boots."

J.B. didn't like it, but the six-guns didn't waver. He sat on the wet ground in the rain and pulled his boots

"Hold 'em upside down and shake 'em."

J.B. did.

"All right." the lawman slowly let the hammer down on his six-gun. "Keep your gun on 'im, Dan," he said to a lanky rider who sported a deputy's badge. He mounted his horse and reached down for the blue-roan's reins. "Get your boots on and climb back in that saddle," he said to J.B. "You're goin' to show us just where you found this stuff—or where you left the body. You tell us the way. I'll lead your horse."

"It's a long ways back," J.B. said. "Six or eight miles."

The lawman thought that over.

"It will be dark before we can get there, sheriff," the big man said.

J.B. took a longer look at the big man and saw that he was dressed in more expensive clothes than the others: striped pants, a gray vest with a gold-colored watch chain draped from the left-side pocket to the right side, and a gray hat that looked new. At first glance he appeared to be a wealthy rancher, but after a longer look, J.B. noticed that his face and hands weren't sun browned the way a rancher's would be.

"All right," the sheriff said, "we'll go back to town and lock this feller up. Tomorrow we're goin' to figure this thing out. He's goin' to tell us all about it, ain't you, young feller?"

"Lock me up?" J.B. couldn't believe it. "What for? I didn't hurt nobody."

"I'm holdin' you on suspicion of murder, young feller," the sheriff said.

"Murder? I didn't even see nobody."

"Get on that horse."

J.B. looked at the faces of the four men and at the two pistols pointed his way. "This is crazy. I'm tellin' you, Mr. Sheriff, I don't like bein' locked up. I don't take kindly to this kind of treatment."

"Get on that horse." The sheriff drew his gun again and cocked the hammer back to emphasize his order. Reluctantly, J.B. mounted the blue-roan. He felt strange and helpless without the reins. He weighed his chances of escape and decided he had no chance at all. He rode in silence awhile, then muttered to himself, "There ain't one chance in a thousand of this happenin' to anybody. Not one chance in a million."

"What'd you say?"

"Nothin'."

CHAPTER 2

It was another five miles east and a little north to the town of El Rey, and when they started down a long hill on the town's west side, J.B. could see why the town was built. It was the railroad.

The most prominent feature was the railroad stock pens on the west side, filled with longhorn cattle, obviously ready to be shipped to a packing house or feedlot someplace.

El Rey itself consisted of one main street and two other streets paralleling the railroad. As they rode down the street, J.B. saw a livery stable on one end and an adobe building with a bank sign at the other end. In between were various clapboard buildings, including the Red Dog Saloon, a general store, a two-story hotel, and another adobe building with a sign over the boardwalk telling everyone that this was the sheriff's office and jail.

The clapboard buildings had false fronts, and roofs that hung over the boardwalks. The roofs were supported by two-by-fours and thin pine timbers from the mountains to the west.

The group dismounted in front of the sheriff's office. At least the office was dry, even though it was unheated. J.B. was told that his horse would be fed at the livery stable. But, the sheriff warned, ol' Tobias at the livery stable had the right to sell the horse and take his bill out of the proceeds if J.B. couldn't pay it. The sheriff chuckled. "From the looks of that hungry-lookin', long-backed brute, if he stays there more'n a few days ol' Tobias'll lose money. The saddle's a good one though. Where'd you steal it?"

J.B. was angry. His emotions, when they had started for El Rey, had been a mixture of anger and fear, but by the time they got there, he was thoroughly angry. Hell, he hadn't done anything wrong. Who in the humped-up world wouldn't have picked up that slicker and money poke if they'd come across it? Hell, he had almost decided to turn it over to the law anyway.

"That blue-roan can carry a man farther and faster than any horse I've ever known," he said, his temper at boiling point, "and that saddle was made to order for me in Fort Worth. Cost me more'n two months' wages. And I'm gonna tell you somethin', Mr. Sheriff, I didn't harm nobody, and if you or anybody sells my horse and outfit, I'm damn sure gonna harm somebody."

He was given a hard shove into the jail cell by the big man, and the cell door was slammed shut and locked. "Tough-talking little rooster, aren't you," the big man said. "You're going to look good dangling on the end of a rope."

J.B. told him where he could go and what he could do when he got there. They left, closing the door between the office and the jail behind them. J.B. looked around. He was alone in a cell with two steel bunks without mattresses or blankets, and a bucket in the corner he could use for a toilet. One narrow window, too narrow for even a boy to squeeze through, provided the only light in the cell. It was dusk outside and the light was dim. The window was above J.B.'s head.

J.B. paced the plank floor awhile, then sat on one of the bunks and held his face in his hands.

"What now?" he asked himself aloud. "How'n the humped-up hell did I git in this pickle?" He stood up and rattled the steel door as if to assure himself he wasn't dreaming, and sat back down. He had been in his share of bad situations before. Any man who drifts around the country the way he did was bound to get into a few jackpots whether he wanted to or not. There had been a few barroom fist fights, and once he had been shot at by a jealous husband. He didn't know the woman was married. And another time he had to use a singletree as a club to persuade a bully to stop picking on him. Now he was accused of murder, and he didn't even know who he was supposed to have killed.

He rolled a cigarette, smoked awhile, then stood up again, gave the cell door a kick, and went back to pacing. He let out a string of obscenities, using both English and cowboy Spanish. He started with the sheriff's grandfather, calling him a *tonto cabrón*, turned next to the sheriff's father, and ended up calling the sheriff and his three cohorts long-headed apes with cow manure for brains. The door between the sheriff's office and the jail opened, and the sheriff approached.

J.B. glared at him, fists clenched, ready to fight. But the sheriff hadn't heard the insults, and he asked matter-of-factly, "You et?"

J.B. opened his mouth to repeat the insults, then decided it would serve no purpose. He said nothing.

"Well, no prisoner of mine is goin' to starve," the sheriff said. "I'm sendin' over to Winters' Cafe for somethin' to eat, and I'll get you a sandwich." He started to leave, then turned back. "We done you a favor lockin' you up. You didn't have a nickel in your pockets."

The sandwich was a good one, a thick slice of roast beef between two slices of homemade bread, and J.B. hadn't eaten all day. He devoured it. Then he smoked his second cigarette since being locked up, and noticed that he had about enough tobacco for one more smoke. He walked the wooden floor again and finally lay back on a bunk with his hat under his head for a pillow. The hat would be crushed, but it was made of good beaver fur and would straighten itself out again. It took only a few minutes for the steel slats to become unbearable. J.B. gave up trying to rest, and walked the floor again.

One more smoke, he thought, and then he would go crazy. It was bad enough being locked up. Locked up with no tobacco would have him grabbing at flies where there weren't any. He picked up the butts from the floor, tore them apart, and salvaged enough unburned tobacco to roll another cigarette. He smoked it until it burned his fingers, then had to drop it. That was when he heard the commotion in the sheriff's office.

"You can't go in there, Miss Crandall." It was the sheriff's voice, but it lacked authority.

"I want to see him." It was a young woman's voice. "I want to see what he looks like. I want to know what he did with Uncle Len's body and where the rest of the money is."

16

"Now now, Miss Crandall. We'll find out all about it in the mornin'. That is, if he did it. He could be tellin' the truth, you know."

"I'll find out," the young woman said. "I'll know if he's telling the truth."

"You can't go in there, Miss Crandall." The sheriff's voice was rising. "It's no place for a lady."

"I'm going in there." The door burst open.

At first, J.B. thought he had been mistaken about the voice. It wasn't a young woman. It was a young man. A very young man. Even smaller than he was.

He, she, or whatever it was, stepped up to the cell door and stood there, hands on hips, spraddle legged. It was wearing a wide-brimmed hat pulled low, a checkered shirt, vest, Levi's, boots and spurs. It scowled at J.B. He scowled back.

"What's your name?" it demanded. "None of your business."

They glared at each other. Then it asked, "Did you kill my uncle?"

"I never saw your uncle."

"You're a liar."

"That's easy to say when there's bars between us."

"What would you do if there weren't any bars."

"I'd turn you over my knee and spank you."

"You and whose army?"

They continued scowling at each other. Finally, it shoved the hat back and wiped its forehead with a handkerchief. A lacy handkerchief. Its hair, the part that showed under the hat brim, was yellow blond and J.B. noticed the eyes were blue, although not as pale as his.

The face that had been angry, tough, belligerent, suddenly softened, and worry lines appeared. The shoulders slumped. The eyes looked down at the floor.

J.B. softened too. "Listen, kid. I don't blame you for bein' fightin' mad. I'd be mad too if I thought somebody'd killed one of my relations. Listen, maybe he's still alive. How do you know he's dead if you ain't seen his body?"

The blue eyes looked up, studied him. He decided then that she was a girl. It was the face. Now that anger had left it, it had to be the soft face of a girl. A blond girl with a few freckles across her nose. A pretty girl. A girl in her middle twenties, maybe a couple of years younger than him.

She studied his features. He met her gaze for a moment, then looked down.

"Where are you from, cowboy?"

His gaze lifted. "I had a home in Texas once."

"You're a drifter." It was a statement, not a question.

"Yeah. But I never got a nickel I didn't earn and I never started a job I didn't finish."

She turned to the sheriff who was standing behind her. "It's no crime to be footloose. I don't think he did it."

"Now, Miss Crandall, we've got plenty of reason to hold 'im for questioning. After all, we found Len Crandall's rain slicker and some of the money on 'im."

"Where do you suppose he put the rest of the money?"

"He prob'ly stashed it someplace where he could go back after it. He ain't so dumb as to carry it around. He wouldn't have been wearin' Len's slicker if he'd had one of his own."

"You said he had no gun?"

"No, but he prob'ly stashed that too."

She faced the cowboy again, holding his gaze. "He didn't do it," she said to the sheriff, still looking at J.B. "He's no killer. The man who killed my uncle knew he was carrying money. It had to be someone who knew him." Facing the sheriff again, she added, "This man is just a drifting cowhand. He's harmless."

"Well," the sheriff said, "we'll keep 'im locked up awhile and see what happens. I want 'im to show us where he said he found Len's slicker."

It was a skinny cigarette that J.B. rolled after the girl left. And it was his last. He had smoked since he was big enough to sneak a smoke behind the barn, and soon his whole system cried for another. He walked the floor, he sat on the floor, he sat on the steel slats, he stretched out on the floor, he got up, he walked.

He muttered, "Now I know why a wild animal will chew off its own foot when it's caught in a trap. This is hell."

When daylight came, the cowboy was dozing fitfully. He was

sitting on the wooden floor in a corner with his knees drawn up, his arms folded across them and his head on his arms. He came awake instantly when the door between the sheriff's office and the jail was opened. Every muscle in his body ached.

Breakfast was slid under the cell door. It consisted of three pancakes and a tin cup of black coffee. Then the sheriff was unlocking the door and ordering him out. But first, the sheriff lifted his pistol from its holster, cocked the hammer back, and held it ready in case J.B. tried to run or fight.

The big man, Miss Crandall, and a deputy were waiting at the livery barn when the sheriff brought J.B. up. They had their horses saddled, and someone had put J.B.'s saddle on the blue-roan.

"Now I'm not goin' to handcuff you and I'm not goin' to lead your horse," the sheriff said to J.B. "But if you try to make a run for it, we've got rifles that'll knock you right out of your saddle."

J.B. loosened the cinch on his saddle, shifted the saddle farther up on the horse's withers, and tightened the cinch again.

"Don't you like the way I saddle a horse?" It was the big man asking.

"Nobody can saddle a horse for me," J.B. said. "It'd be like havin' somebody put my hat on for me."

The girl backed him. "Cowboys are like that."

But the big man wanted all present to know he didn't like the cowboy, and didn't trust him. He said, "This runt just wants to make trouble. He killed a man and he's putting on an innocent act, and he figures to ride away from here with thirty thousand in cash. Somebody else's cash."

J.B. dropped the reins on the ground, walked over to the big man and stood in front of him, his eyes narrow and his fists clenched. "What did you call me?"

The big man stood spraddle legged and balled his fists too. The sheriff tried to placate both sides. "Easy, there," he said to J.B. To the big man he said, "We don't know for sure he did it, Mr. Buetel."

Buetel ignored the sheriff. "I called you a runt," he hissed. "A bandy-legged, pin-headed runt."

J.B. knew he couldn't win a slugging match with the big man, but he had been in brawls with big bullies before. Instead of swinging his fists, he kicked.

The hard heel of his riding boot slammed into Buetel's right knee, and the big man's leg collapsed, causing him to stagger forward. The cowboy's right fist met him—squarely on the nose. Then the left fist caught him on the jaw. Then the right to the nose again.

Buetel, surprised by the fury of the onslaught, and hurt, covered his head with both arms and turned, bent over, with his back to J.B., trying to protect his face.

J.B. gave him a kick in the seat of the pants that sent him sprawling.

"Git up, you son of a..." J.B. remembered there was a girl present. "Git up, you big hunk of mutton." Buetel rolled over and sat up slowly. He wiped the back of his hand across his nose and saw it was bloody.

He grabbed for the pistol on his hip.

But the cowboy was expecting that, and he landed with both feet on the big man's gun hand before the gun cleared leather. He reached down and picked up the gun.

Then his head exploded.

He was lying on his back on the ground when his eyes opened. A girl with long blond hair was on her knees beside him. A wet bandanna was being held to the side of his head. J.B. let his eyes wander without moving his head. He saw the sheriff standing at his feet.

"I didn't mean to hit 'im so hard, but he's a murder suspect and I couldn't let 'im get his hands on a gun."

"He was only defending himself," the girl replied. "And you can kill a man with a gun barrel the same as with a bullet."

"Now, Miss Crandall, why don't you go on home and let me and my deputy handle this?"

"I'm going along," she said. "That is, if this man can ride."

"Now, Miss Crandall..." The sheriff said no more.

She saw his eyes were open and she removed the wet bandanna from the side of his head. "Can you sit up?"

He sat up slowly, carefully.

"Good." She held up her right hand, one finger extended. "How many fingers do you see?"

"Two hundred and fifty-four."

"Look again. How many do you see?"

He looked at her face, into her eyes, and managed a lopsided grin. "Okay, only one."

"You'll live," she said, standing up. "On your feet, cowboy."

He stood up and swayed drunkenly for a moment while his head cleared. When his vision steadied, he saw that Buetel was gone. She stepped close, studied the left side of his head, and said, "You'll have some swelling and a sore spot for a day or two, but I don't think you have a concussion."

"Is that somethin' you learned at the university, Miss Crandall?" the sheriff asked. "About concussions?"

"I took a course in home medical care," she said sharply. "I knew it would come in handy on a ranch." She glanced around, at the sheriff, at his deputy, and at J.B. "Get on your horses and let's get started."

J.B. shot a glance at the sheriff and wondered why he was allowing the girl to give orders. The sheriff merely shrugged and picked up his bridle reins.

The girl picked her hat off the ground, gathered her shoulder-length blond hair into a bunch, and held it on top of her head with one hand while she carefully put the hat on. When the hat was in place, it covered her hair, and with her loose fitting shirt and Levi's, J.B. thought she could still be mistaken for a boy.

J.B. put his hat on so that it was tilted to the right, to keep pressure off the sore spot.

"Are you sure you can find the place?" she asked

J.B. as they rode out of town, past the railroad pens.

J.B. saw that the penned longhorn cattle were eating hay, and he wondered idly where the hay had come from.

"I've spent nearly half my life chasing cattle over rougher country than this," he said.

The sheriff and his lanky deputy carried rifles across their saddles, and they flanked J.B. on both sides. "You keep that horse on a steady trot," the sheriff said. "If he breaks into a lope, this

Winchester's goin' to go off aimed right at you."

"I've got nothin' to run from," the cowboy grumbled.

"Don't worry, Sheriff White," the girl said, a small smile playing around the corners of her mouth, "that long-necked Texas horse of his doesn't look like it could outrun a hobbled ho-dad anyway."

J.B. gave her a mean look. "Don't you go pokin' fun at my horse. He didn't cost much, but he's a better horse than he looks."

"What will you do about it?" she taunted, the beginning of a smile still evident. "Kick me in the knee?"

"If I didn't have guns pointed at me I'd consider learnin' you some manners."

"You and whose army?"

They rode in silence for the next half hour, their horses trotting steadily. The girl was becoming uncomfortable with the rough gait, and was standing in her stirrups at times, leaning against the fork of the saddle to relieve the bouncing. The blue-roan, with its longer legs, was taking fewer steps and traveling easily. J.B. was comfortable.

He cleared his throat to get her attention, then grinned broadly at her to show that he was aware of her discomfort and that he, on his awkward-looking mount, was having no problems.

She knew the meaning of his smile, but said nothing and looked straight ahead.

He chuckled at that. She shot him a scowl, but still said nothing.

He found the arroyo, and led the way to the overhanging rock. Without dismounting, he pointed. "Right under there."

Sheriff White and the girl dismounted. The deputy stayed on his horse and kept his rifle pointed at J.B.

"A natural cave," she said. "For thousands of years, water ran down this arroyo. It took that long to erode the soil and rock and create this recession."

"It ain't big enough to keep a man from gettin' wet in a downpour," the sheriff said, "but it'd help." He got down on his hands and knees and poked among the rocks and small crevices between the rocks. "Some strange-lookin' tracks here. Can't figure 'em out." He stood up and walked slowly toward the other end of the ravine, studying the ground. "Horse tracks, but only one horse. Uh oh, here's another'n." He squatted and traced a dim imprint with a forefinger. "Rain almost washed 'em away, but there was another horse down here not long ago."

Still studying the ground, Sheriff White walked slowly back to the group. "One horse stood here awhile. His horse." He pointed at J.B. "'Nother horse stood over there awhile. And it was nervous, stomped around some. This horse stood quiet."

The sheriff took his hat off and scratched his head. His head was nearly bald. "What do you think, Dan?" he asked the deputy.

Dan took his time answering, and when he talked he talked with a slow, lazy drawl. "Wa-al, nothin' could've fell under that rock by accident. If the slicker and poke was ever there, they was put there."

J.B. spoke up. "The strange marks under that rock is where I sat with my bed tarp over my head. I didn't find the slicker 'til I'd been here five, maybe ten minutes. Whoever put it there was tryin' to hide it. There wasn't one chance in a thousand of somebody comin' along and findin' it."

The girl knelt, staring at the horse tracks. "Could the nervous horse have been running, sheriff? I mean, could it have been nervous because it had been running?"

"Could be," Sheriff White answered. "Could it have been Mr. Crandall's horse?" he asked her.

"I don't know. It was shod, but nearly all horses are shod around here, except maybe the big cow outfits' remuda horses. Uncle Len was riding Red Feather, his favorite mount. Red Feather was shod and he's a quiet horse."

"Well," the sheriff gathered his reins and stepped into the saddle, "we didn't learn much here. Except there was another horse besides this'n here, and this here arroyo is maybe a mile away from the wagon road Mr. Crandall would've taken to town." He was quiet a moment, thinking, then, "If Mr. Crandall was here, it's because somebody forced him here with a gun."

"Or chased him here," J.B. put in.

Squinting at the cowboy, the sheriff asked, "What makes you say that, young feller?"

"It's what the lady said. A runnin' horse that's pulled to a stop ain't gonna quiet down for a few seconds. If somebody was chasin' somebody and he rode down here to hide, well..." J.B. shrugged.

"It could be," the sheriff said. "But the other thing could be too. It could be he was forced down here with a gun and shot and robbed."

"If that there's the case," drawled the deputy, "his body has to be around here sommers. The killer couldn't carry a dead body very fur."

"We were all over this part of the county yesterday," the sheriff said. "We rode down every arroyo and looked behind every tree. 'Course, a man's body is easy to hide." Sheriff White lifted his hat and scratched his nearly bald head again. "All the killer'd have to do is roll a body into one of these thousand shallow draws and cover it with rocks and a man would have to ride right over it to see it."

The deputy started rolling a smoke, and J.B.'s hand automatically went to his shirt pocket in search of his own tobacco. His spirits, already low, dropped a few more notches when he remembered he was out. His eyes hungrily followed the deputy's hand as a match was struck and the cigarette was lighted. He had to swallow the saliva in his throat as the deputy exhaled, blowing smoke. The girl noticed the pained expression on his face.

"Yep," the sheriff was saying, "we might never find that body. The coyotes will have the bones scattered all over the county." Then he remembered the girl and apologized. "I'm sorry, Miss Crandall. I didn't mean to, uh,..." He ran his fingers through his sparse hair again.

J.B. considered asking for a smoke. The deputy would probably give him the makin's. But no. These men were no friends of his, and he'd be damned if he'd beg for anything. They could all go to hell. He swallowed again and tried to concentrate on what was being said.

The sheriff was talking. "What I mean, Miss Crandall, is, don't be surprised if we never find Len Crandall's body. There's just too much country and too many hiding places."

J.B. squinted from under his broad hat brim at the sheriff and said with a touch of disgust in his voice, "If it's hidden in one of these 'royos, anybody can find it."

"What do you mean?" the sheriff asked, irritably. "If they covered a body with rocks they'd have to pick up a lot of rocks, wouldn't they? Anybody could see where they'd done that."

"And what about Red Feather, the horse?" Miss Crandall

interjected. "A horse's body wouldn't be so easy to hide. And if Red Feather were turned loose, he would go back to the ranch."

"It ain't always so," put in Deputy Dan. "A horse raised in a barn might go back to the barn, but a horse raised in the hills might go back to his favorite grazin' land, or maybe he'd drift 'till he saw a bunch of grazin' horses and join 'em."

Sheriff White put his hat back in place and squinted at the horizon. "He'll prob'ly turn up in somebody's remuda, or he's croppin' the grass with your mares and colts," he said to the girl.

J.B. spoke again. "Can I say somethin', sheriff?"

The sheriff was still irritated. "You ain't been bashful yet."

"If somebody was killed and his horse stolen, then the horse was led away to Santa Fe or Taos or Raton. I rode up from Santa Fe yesterday and I didn't see nobody, so the horse is prob'ly in Raton right now. Find that horse and you'll get an idea who killed that man—if he was killed."

"You said you rode up from Santa Fe yesterday," the sheriff said, "but Mr. Crandall disappeared three days ago. That horse could be anywhere."

J.B. looked at the ground and shook his head in disbelief. "Then what in hell—excuse me ma'am—what makes you think I could've killed 'im? Do you think I could've killed a man three days ago and hung around all that long?"

"No-o," Sheriff White spoke slowly, considering every word. "No, but what could have happened is, you rode up from Santa Fe, saw Mr. Crandall, figured out he had money in his saddlebags, shot him, hid the saddlebags, took the horse back to Santa Fe and sold 'im, then came back for the money."

The sheriff squinted at J.B. "I'm not sayin' that's exactly what happened, young feller. But you have to admit it could have happened that way."

J.B. couldn't believe what he was hearing. "That's crazy. That's the craziest thing I ever heard of." He looked at the three people around him, one at a time. The sheriff and the deputy met his gaze, stern expressions on their faces. The girl looked down.

"I think we'd better make a trip to Santa Fe," the sheriff said to his deputy. "This young feller did get one thing right: if we find that horse, we'll have a better idea of what happened."

"Why Santa Fe?" J.B. asked, his voice rising. "Why not Taos or Raton? Hell—excuse me, lady—if somebody killed this Mr. Crandall and took his horse, he could of gone west or north instead of south."

The sheriff answered him first by again pointing his rifle at him. "You don't seem to want us to go to Santa Fe, do you, young feller? Well, that's a pretty good reason for goin'. And in the meantime, we're takin' you back to town and lockin' you up again. I'm gettin' more suspicious of you all the time."

J.B. had had enough. He was tired of being accused of a murder he knew nothing about, he was tired of trying to help solve a crime when he didn't even know who was killed or if anyone had even been killed, and he was tired of being a prisoner with guns pointed at him. Besides, his head hurt where he had been hit with a gun barrel.

"Aw, go whistle up a rope, you lame-brained old buzzard. The people that elected you sheriff have to be as dumb as you are and you're so dumb you don't know sic 'em from love 'em and I'll tell you somethin' else, sooner or later you're gonna find out I didn't do no wrong and you're gonna have to turn me loose and when you do I'm gonna kick your ass—excuse me, lady—I'm gonna kick your tail 'til you bark like a fox."

Sheriff White poked him in the ribs with the barrel of his rifle. "Keep runnin' off at the mouth, young feller, and I'm goin' to enjoy hangin' you."

Miss Crandall interjected, "He has a point. You really have no solid evidence against him, sheriff."

"Would you want me to send 'im on his way?" the sheriff asked.

She took her time answering, gazing at the horizon.

"No, I guess not. I guess he ought to be held until we find Uncle Len's body or his horse or something."

J.B. scowled at her. "You can go whistle up a rope too."

"Get goin'," the sheriff ordered.

J.B. rode out of the arroyo and headed toward El Rey with two guns pointed at him.

CHAPTER 3

If they had been in the timber he might have made a break for it. He might have been able to keep enough trees between him and the guns to be a poor target, and he believed his blue-roan gelding could outdistance their horses in an endurance race. But out in the open country he didn't have a chance. Even a blind man couldn't miss hitting either him or his horse with a rifle bullet.

He had little faith in the law or lawmen. He had seen too much injustice. He was worried. In fact, he was scared. Men had been hung for crimes they didn't commit. And he knew that drifters, even though they may be honest, hard-working men, were considered by many lawmen and townspeople to be nothing better than bums whose lives didn't matter much anyway. He had seen it in the Texas farm country as a youngster. When the cotton needed harvesting and the farmers were looking for "boll pullers," the itinerant workers were welcomed with open arms. But when the harvest was over, it was "Git out of town."

J.B.'s mind was going over bitter thoughts, and he was tense, looking for a chance to clap spurs to the blue-roan and race away. But finally he forced himself to relax and await his fate. He was better off trusting to luck, he figured, than trying to outrun rifle bullets. Or was he? "How," he muttered almost inaudibly, "can one man have so much rotten luck in one week?"

"What'd you say, young feller?"

"Nothin'."

Again the cell door clanged shut, and again J.B. was advised that his horse and saddle, everything he owned, could be sold if he couldn't pay the livery stable.

And again, J.B. walked the floor trying to find a shred of tobacco he could use. He managed to pinch off a tiny bit that had not been burned, and in desperation he put it in his mouth and chewed it, hoping that would help sate his hunger. "Gaw-ud," he groaned aloud, "I'd give a month's wages for a sack of Bull Durham."

Then the connecting door opened and Miss Crandall was standing before his cell, handing him a sack of tobacco between the bars. "I guessed from the hungry look on your face that you were out of makings. I can imagine how it must be."

Her generosity so surprised J.B. that he could only mumble his thanks, and she was gone again before he could say all that he thought he ought to say.

The cigarette, when he had it rolled and lighted, helped calm his nerves, and he began to worry again. He smoked three cigarettes, one after the other. He walked. He cussed.

Could he break out of jail? Men had broken out of jail before. How? Every time the cell door was opened, the sheriff had his six-gun in his hand and the hammer back. Dig out? With what? They had searched his pockets and taken his folding knife. The floor planks were thick and solid. J.B. looked around for something he could use as a digging tool or prying tool or anything. There wasn't one *chingao* thing. He looked up at the window. Nobody could squeeze through that.

If he had friends on the outside maybe they could help. But hell, he had no friends. Not in El Rey. And if he did manage to run, he would be a fugitive, and he would always be looking over his shoulder and trying to go the other way every time he saw a lawman. Still, that would be better than being locked up. Any damn thing is better than this, he thought.

He reached a decision. He would watch for a chance. He would risk a bullet in the back if he had to. One thing was certain: he was not going to stay locked up like a caged animal. Not for very long.

"Goddam lawmen," he muttered. "Give 'em a badge and build 'em a jail and they just have to lock somebody up. I knew there was a reason I never liked lawmen."

Just before dark, a meal of beans and beef stew was brought to him. He ate. He smoked. He lay on the steel bunk and managed to sleep for a short time—until the steel slats became so uncomfortable he could no longer lie on them.

He walked the floor, he sat, he smoked, he slept a few more minutes. Finally, daylight could be seen in the narrow window.

The sheriff brought him a plate of biscuits and water gravy for breakfast, and told him that jail inmates got only two meals a day, and that since he was a broke drifter, he was lucky to get that. The meal had cooled since it had left the kitchen, but J.B. ate it anyway. The sheriff came back for the plate.

"I'm goin' down to Santa Fe," Sheriff White said. "I won't get back 'til tomorrow, but when I do I expect to know more about what happened to Mr. Crandall. If I find that horse and find out somebody that don't fit your description had 'im, I might consider turnin' you loose."

"What you ought to do," J.B. said, "is ask the gamblers and the bartender in the Muy Bonita saloon if they remember me bein' there the day your Mr. Crandall disappeared. That ought to prove I had nothin' to do with it."

"I might do that," Sheriff White said. "Yessir, if I have time I might do that."

"If you have time? Listen, you..." J.B. considered, then rejected the idea of calling the sheriff what he should be called. "If you're concerned at all with justice like a lawman's supposed to be, you'll damn well find time."

"I'll think about it," the sheriff said, and left.

J.B. never felt so helpless or so frustrated in his life. He knew how to prove his innocence, but he was denied the opportunity to do it. He had to depend on some adle-brained sheriff politician who was no doubt better at getting votes than at solving crimes.

Breaking out of jail seemed even more important now than it did the day before. If only he could find a way. Hell he had to find a way.

J.B. found that by standing on a corner of the steel bunk and stretching every muscle in his body he could see out the narrow window overhead. The wood frame building next to the jail blocked his view of all but a small slice of the street, though he could see for half a block down the alley. A few men walked past on the boardwalk. Once he saw a woman go past, dragging a small boy by the arm. The town was quiet.

It was another deputy who brought in J.B.'s midafternoon meal. He was one of the four who had accosted J.B. out on the road to town, a narrow, thin man with a drooping moustache and a prominent adam's apple. He shoved the tin plate of boiled potatoes and fried beef under the cell bars and walked away without saying a word. J.B. watched him leave, then picked up the plate and the bent fork that was with it, tasted the food, made a wry face, and ate it all.

The sun was still shining between the adobe jail and the wooden building next door when the commotion started.

Loud voices came from the alley. Angry voices. Men's voices. J.B. stood on the bunk, stretched as high as he could and peered out the narrow window. Men were gathered in the alley, looking his way.

"Hey, you," one of them shouted. "You in the jail. We wanta talk to you." The man had a derby hat on his head and wore baggy pants held up with red suspenders. The crowd, consisting of about fifteen men and a woman, moved in a bunch to the window. Many of the men wore range clothes, and one had a Box O brand painted on his chaps.

"Ol' Len was a good friend of these boys," Derby flat said, "and they're fightin' mad over him bein' murdered and robbed."

"What'd you do with the body?" a cowboy asked. "We oughta hang you by the neck," yelled another man. A loud murmur of agreement came from the crowd. "Hell, yes, hang 'im," someone yelled. "Git a rope."

"I got a brand new catch rope," shouted the cowboy with the Box O chaps. "It ain't never been used and it needs a good stretchin'."

Someone else shouted, "There's an old piss-ellum tree 'crost the alley that's got a stout limb about twenty feet high."

"Hang 'im."

"Yeah, but first we oughta notch his ears and brand his butt and make 'im tell us where he hid the body." It was Derby Hat yelling. The crowd was getting louder, shouting agreement.

30

"Listen," J.B. said, his face as close to the window as he could get. "I never even saw anyone comin' up here. There's people in Santa Fe that can tell you I was down there two-three days ago when that Mr. Crandall was supposed to've disappeared."

"You're a liar." It was Derby Hat again. The man turned to the crowd. "He's just makin' that up. Hell, he was found wearin' Len's slicker and carryin' some of his gold. He's a back-shootin' killer and we can't wait for no circuit judge to come up here and tell us what to do with 'im."

A woman with scraggly hair and a tooth missing in the front of her face shouted in a whisky-husky voice, "He's cute. He'll look real nice with his neck stretched and his tongue hangin' out."

"Ol Len was crazy, but he wasn't a bad hombre to work for," yelled a man with a flat-brim hat and bib overalls. "We cain't let his killer git away with it."

Another put in: "All them judges do nowadays is send 'em to the pen for a couple of years, and then they git out and kill somebody else."

"We can put a stop to his killin' right now," came another voice.

"Hang 'im." The voice came from the center of the crowd.

"Tell you what, boys," Derby Hat said. "Come on over to the Red Dog and I'll buy a round and we'll talk this over."

Someone laughed with a loud "Haw-haw. Let's hold court ourselves." Another laugh. "Yeah, then hang 'im legal."

Derby Hat lead the way past the window and onto the boardwalk, and the crowd followed, laughing, cursing, and looking back at J.B. Someone threw a rock, but it hit the wall harmlessly, two feet from J.B.'s face.

J.B. dropped down from the steel bunk and stood there, muttering to himself. "Well, that leads the goddam parade. No matter how bad everything gits, it can always git worse. Am I gonna be hung for a killin' I never had nothin' to do with?"

He paced the floor, sat on the bunk, smoked, paced. His heart leaped into his throat when the door between the sheriff's office and the jail opened. His first thought was the mob had come for him. But when he saw what entered, he was puzzled.

She was a little old lady, wearing a sunbonnet that covered her head and most of her face and a long-sleeved gingham dress that was so long it dragged on the floor. She carefully closed the door and walked up to J.B.'s cell. He recognized her then.

"Shhh," said Miss Crandall. She produced a key, opened the cell door, and shoved a bundle of clothes at him. "Put these on and hurry. You have to get out of there. Those men are getting drunker and nastier."

He unrolled the bundle of clothes and was puzzled again. It was a long dress, like the one Miss Crandall was wearing, and a bonnet, also like the one she was wearing.

"Hurry," she urged. "You have to have a disguise to get out of here. The sheriff and his chief deputy aren't here, and that deputy hasn't got gumption enough to hold them back."

He tried to step into the dress. "No, dummy, over your head," she whispered. J.B. found the bottom of the dress and slipped it over his head. It was a struggle, but he finally got his arms in the sleeves.

"Button the top," she said.

He started to button it, then had an idea and stuffed his black hat inside the bodice before fastening the rest of the buttons. When he was finished, he was covered from his neck to the floor. The long dress even hid his boots and spurs.

"Put on that bonnet." She laid the key on one of the bunks. "I stole it. There's nobody in the sheriff's office now. Put that on and let's get out of here."

J.B. fumbled with the bonnet, trying to figure out how to put it on. She grabbed it out of his hands, slammed it onto his head, and tied it under his chin. "Do I have to dress you?" she said. The cowboy started to protest, but thought better of it.

"Come on," she said.

He followed her to the connecting door, which she opened carefully. After peering into the outer room, she whispered, "Follow me. I've got your horse down the street." She stopped just before she opened the outer door, and glanced back at him. The beginning of a smile played around the corners of her mouth again. "Try to walk like a lady, will you."

He looked down at himself and had a sudden urge to laugh. But the fear of being caught drove the urge away.

The sun looked to be two hours above the horizon when they started down the boardwalk. Traffic on the street was light, and they received only a few curious glances. J.B. walked carefully and was doing all right until he tripped on the hem of the dress and almost fell. A cowboy riding past turned his head to look at him.

"Oh, my goodness, Aunt Martha, said Miss Crandall in a false voice, "a body could break a leg on these awful sidewalks."

The cowboy rode on.

The blue-roan was tied to the hitchrail beside Miss Crandall's bay horse in front of the livery barn. J.B. untied the reins and had to lift the skirt to get his boot in the stirrup. When he swung aboard, his pant legs, boots, and spurs showed beneath the dress.

Miss Crandall was wearing boots and spurs too and they also showed when she mounted her horse.

The stableman, a skinny fellow with a floppy hat, stood with his mouth open, glancing from him to her and back to him. J.B. kept looking back at the Red Dog Saloon. He half expected to hear a shout and see a bloodthirsty mob come boiling out.

They rode at a slow gallop until they got out of town, past the stockyards still filled with longhorn cattle, and were headed west toward the timber country. Then she reined her horse to a stop, looked back, and saw no one behind them. She looked over at J.B. and chuckled.

It was a polite titter at first, and she apologized. "I'm sorry, but you're the funniest sight I ever saw." He couldn't understand how anyone could laugh at such a narrow escape from hanging. Then he looked down at himself and he had to chuckle.

Her titter turned into laughter. "You've even got a big bosom." Her laughter was contagious, and although he felt like a desperado, he had to laugh with her. He took off the bonnet, unbuttoned the bodice, took out his hat, reshaped it, and put it on his head. The more she laughed, the more he laughed. They both whooped and haw-hawed. Suddenly, she looked behind them and her laughter ceased.

"Uh oh, they're wise to us. They're coming."

He saw them. There were six or seven of them, riding at a dead run. Derby Hat was on a gray horse in the lead.

What happened next was a horse race.

At first, Miss Crandall's cow pony jumped out ahead of the blue-roan—the short-backed horse had a quicker burst of speed—but after three hundred yards, the longer-legged horse caught up and J.B. had to hold him back to keep him from running away from the girl.

"Keep going," she shouted as J.B. rode alongside. "Get yourself away from here. They'll hang you."

"I cain't leave you to that pack of hounds," he shouted back.

"Don't worry about me. They won't bother me. I...my family has some influence around here."

"You saved my life. I cain't leave you behind." The wind was whipping the long dress over his knees.

"I'll be all right, I promise. Come to the CC Ranch tonight. Go straight ahead about six miles to Juniper Creek. Go up stream about three more miles and you'll come to the ranch. You'll see the CC brand painted on the side of the barn. Come to the house. I'll be looking for you."

"Are you sure you'll be all right?"

"I promise. Now go."

J.B. pitched the slack to the blue-roan and the tall horse pulled away, not only from the girl but from the pursuers as well. J.B. reined the horse off the road and headed north, toward the high country. She watched him go, and as she brought her horse to a stop, she shouted, "Remind me not to make fun of that horse again."

Two of the pursuers stopped beside her and the others kept going after J.B. She untied the bonnet, slipped it off her head, and shook out her blond hair. She smiled, "You seem to be in a hurry, Joel."

A tall, lean, young cowboy with a square-jawed face reined his prancing horse around in front of her. "Well, for... Why'd you do that, Miss Crandall? Why'd you help that feller get away?"

She hooked one leg over the saddle horn, unmindful that her bare knee was showing above the boot top. The cowboy glanced at her knee and quickly looked away, embarrassed. She smiled at his embarrassment. "How long have you worked for the CC, Joel?" she asked.

"Since I was a kid."

"Then you know me well enough to know I sometimes do strange things."

"But," he said, uncertainty in his voice, "that feller killed ol' Len."

"Are you sure about that, Joel?"

"They said he did."

"Who said?"

"Mr. Buetel, and Dutch Schultz, and Jake Landers, the bartender."

"Do you believe everything you hear in the Red Dog Saloon?"

He answered weakly, "No, but..."

"You might have hung an innocent man, Joel." She looked into his face. "Now aren't you glad I saved you from that?"

Frown wrinkles appeared between his eyes. "Well, yes, Shine—uh, Miss Crandall."

"It's all right. You can call me Shine."

His face brightened. She put both feet in the stirrups and rode away at a walk. He followed. The other man, who had been quiet up to that moment, stayed behind and said after them, "My horse is too fat for that kind of work. I'll see you later."

The blue-roan was tiring and blowing hard when it carried J.B. over a low, rocky ridge. J.B. brought the horse to a stop just under the ridge, dismounted, and walked back to the top, bending low. He crouched beside a piñon and studied his back trail. The men were so far behind he could barely see them. He could see, however, that they had stopped.

The race was over.

After loosening the cinches on his saddle, allowing the horse to rest a little easier, the cowboy went back to the top of the ridge, lay on his stomach, and watched his pursuers. He grunted with satisfaction when he saw them turn around and go back the way they had come, riding at a slow walk. He lay there until they were completely out of sight, then stood up. He tore off the long dress, wadded it up, and covered it with rocks. His close brush with a hanging party made him pensive, and he worked silently. When he finished, he noticed that the pile of rocks looked like a small grave, and he grinned to himself when he thought about how, one day, someone would see it and wonder what it was. Chuckling, he imagined the scene: A cowboy might be driving a bunch of cows over the ridge, a cow would accidentally kick one of the rocks out of place, the cowboy would see a piece of the dress, dismount, uncover it carefully, almost afraid of what he might find, pick up the dress, shake it out, and spend the rest of the day and half the night trying to figure out how a woman's dress happened to be covered with rocks on top of a ridge a long way from any settlement.

J.B. took his lass rope off the saddle and looped it around the horse's neck. He pulled the saddle and bridle off and let the horse graze with no encumbrances. He knew he could catch the animal as long as it had a rope around its neck.

The sun had not yet set in the west when storm clouds gathered in the high country to the north and west. Lightning cut a jagged line across the western sky. J.B. guessed that the storm would move down onto the rocky flats before dark, and he was right.

When it came, he was huddled under his bed tarp with his saddle and bridle. He kept dry and kept his equipment dry. He even dozed awhile. The horse wasn't bothered by the rain and it continued grazing happily.

The storm lasted about an hour and quit almost as suddenly as if someone had turned off a spigot. The sun had gone down by then, but there was still enough daylight left for J.B. to see a small stream at the bottom of the ridge, a stream that hadn't been there before.

The cowboy rolled up the bed tarp and allowed as how the rain would make the grass grow. "This has to be mighty good cow country," he said to himself. He saddled the horse and was ready to leave. But then he had to make a decision.

Should he find the CC Ranch and the girl, as she had asked him to? Or should he just ride? Head back to Texas. He owed her his life. That mob intended to hang him. And like she said, that deputy didn't have gumption enough to stop them. She acted like a woman in trouble, more trouble than just losing an uncle can cause. She was kind of strange, when he thought about it. At times she looked to be under a hell of a load, and at the same time she could laugh easily.

She had asked him to come to the ranch, and that meant she needed his help. Why, J.B. couldn't imagine. But he owed her. Besides, if he drifted, he'd be a wanted man.

He guessed that Sheriff White wouldn't even try to unravel the mystery of the missing rancher as long as J.B. was at large. And dammit, he wasn't guilty. J.B.'s anger was rising to the surface. He might have done something dumb by not putting that gold and that slicker right back where he found it, but he was no criminal.

Yet those townspeople and cowhands had wanted to hang him. Had it not been for the girl, whose uncle he was supposed to have murdered, his body would be hanging by the neck from a tree right now. "Why, those bloodthirsty, booze-happy sons of..." The more he thought about it, the angrier J.B. became. "I could be dead right now," he muttered to himself. "Hung for a murder I know nothin' about. And my brothers and friends would never even know what happened to me. Why, those stump-headed sons of..."

J.B. gathered his reins and stepped into the saddle.

CHAPTER 4

The horse could see much better in the dark than the cowboy could, and J.B. let it find its own way over the rocks. He was headed back the way he had come. Back to El Rey.

He let the blue-roan take its time, knowing he would need its strength and speed again before the night was over. "I hate to tell you this, Ol' Amigo," he said, "but I've got more work for you."

He stopped on a hill overlooking the stockyards and the main street. Clouds had drifted away to the east, and a full moon lighted up the terrain. J.B. could see the longhorn cattle standing or lying in the railroad pens, and about a dozen saddled horses tied to a hitchrack in front of the town's one saloon. Light came out of both the saloon and the sheriff's office and jail.

A cowhand staggered through the saloon's batwing doors, stumbled to the hitchrack, untied a horse, and climbed awkwardly onto its back. The horse waited patiently until its rider was in the saddle, then moved at a slow trot down the street and out of town.

"It's a good thing his horse is gentle," J.B. said to himself. "or that cowboy would be standing on his head."

A woman's laughter came out of the saloon, and J.B. imagined it was the stringy-haired, snaggle-toothed woman who had wanted to hang him. He was already angry, and her laughter angered him even more.

"So you want some excitement, do you?" he said, as he turned the blue-roan toward the stock pens. "Just stick around."

He made his way quietly to the pens and opened the largest gate, the one nearest town. He rode in. The longhorns snorted at him, and those lying down jumped to their feet. "You're fat and feelin' good, ain't you, and wantin' to git out of here," J.B. said. "Now's your chance."

When the cattle nearest the gate saw it was open, they poured out. Their horns made a clacking noise as they knocked together. The rest followed, and soon twelve hundred longhorn cattle were free. J.B. had been working as quietly as possible until then. Then he untied the bed tarp from behind the cattle, rode at a slow gallop up to the head of the herd—and started a stampede.

Whooping and yelling, he waved the tarp in the faces of the lead steers and got them turned toward the main street. As if on cue, the longhorns, which had been ambling easily up until then, jumped into a wild, uncontrolled run. They ran blindly, crazily, trampling every bush and small tree in their way. J.B., still whooping like a drunk Indian, urged them on, waving the tarp and making them think the devil himself was after them.

The leaders veered away from the town and headed south, and J.B. spurred the blue-roan to catch up to them. He rode hard, recklessly, knowing that if his horse stumbled and fell he would be trampled to death. He caught the leaders and, popping the tarp in their faces, got them turned back in the direction he wanted them to go: right down the main street of El Rey.

They were a swirling, storming mass of bony backs, reds, browns, and brindles, with horns sticking up out of the mass. They were a tornado, thunder, cannon fire, and flood all in one. Everything gave way before them.

It was all J.B. had hoped for. The stampeding longhorns turned the boardwalks to splinters. Two-by-fours and timbers supporting roofs over the boardwalks were flattened, and the roofs came down onto the backs of steers. The longhorns immediately tossed pieces of roof through glass windows.

The racket drew a handful of men outside the saloon. Among them was the man in the derby hat and red suspenders. When they saw what was coming, they let out a series of squawks and warning yells and dove back inside. The woman who had laughed only a few moments earlier began screaming hysterically. Glass was smashed, roofs crashed to the ground, horses tied to the hitchrail broke their reins and stampeded themselves ahead of the longhorns. One horse couldn't break its tie rope, but it snapped the hitchrail and dragged a length of it down the street. A team of horses hitched to a light wagon stampeded along with the rest. When the doubletree broke, the team went straight ahead while the wagon turned crazily and crashed through the door of the Piñon Valley National Bank.

J.B. reined the blue-roan to a stop on the edge of town and watched the destruction. He laughed. He whooped and haw-hawed. "Try to hang me, will you, you bunch of rattlesnakes." He laughed so hard tears ran down his face.

Two steers were crowded through the door of the Red Dog Saloon, and J.B. could hear furniture being wrecked and bottles breaking as the terrified animals fought their way out again, right through the glass window. The woman's screams picked up an octave, and J.B. guessed that her racket was as hard for the saloon patrons to put up with as anything else.

And finally they were gone, leaving pieces of boardwalk, roofs, and broken glass all over the street. Main Street was a shambles.

When the last of the longhorns disappeared, the only horses left in El Rey were those in the livery stable's feed lot. About a dozen horses milled inside the lot. A gate close to the main street was broken and tilted, but it was still standing.

J.B. was disappointed at that. If those horses could be run off, the whole town would be left afoot. He chuckled when he thought of how helpless a cowboy is without a horse, and how everyone would be trying to catch a mount. It occurred to J.B. that the gate could be pulled down. And, if it was pulled down, the horses, already excited by the longhorn stampede, would immediately leave town. He unfastened the lass rope on his saddle.

Dare he? Men were gathering on the street, looking over the wreckage. If he did it, he would have to move fast. Should he?

Hell, yes.

He clapped spurs to the blue-roan and rode at a dead run down into the town, building a loop in his rope at the same time. He rode past two men, who stared after him with open mouths. By the time he reached the livery stable, he had a loop built and was whirling it over his head to put some power behind it. He pitched it.

The loop shot with a Texas roper's accuracy around an upright corner of the gate. J.B. halted the blue-roan a half second, took two quick dallies around his saddle horn, and rode on. The strength of the blue-roan jerked the gate off its hinges, and the penned horses stampeded out.

Men shouted, trying to head them off. It was useless. The horses ran right past them and headed for open country. The town of El Rey was afoot.

J.B. heard a shot and guessed it was aimed at him. He had no time to retrieve his rope. He allowed the end to slip off the saddle horn and rode hard for the hill on the west side of town, back the way he had come.

Behind him were shouting, cursing men, a screaming barroom woman, and a shambles of a town.

When J.B. topped the hill, he stopped, looked back, and saw no pursuers. It was possible that someone had a horse or two in a private corral somewhere back of the main street, but it was not likely. The full moon was putting out enough light that J.B. could see down into the town clearly, and there were no horses. He was almost certain he could take his time leaving. He let the blue-roan blow awhile, then rode on at a mile-eating trot in the same direction he'd traveled earlier that day.

Exactly when he had decided, he wasn't sure, but he realized he was following the directions the girl had given him to the CC Ranch. "Let's see," he said to himself, "about six miles ahead to a creek, then three miles north. That ought to put me on the other side of those mesas I saw and close to the rim of that range of mountains." He reached down and scratched the blue-roan's neck. "I apologize for all this night ridin', Ol' Amigo." He chuckled. "You might not know it, but you've got a desperado on your back."

Juniper Creek was easy to follow the first mile, but farther upstream, where the creek wound its way through the rocky foothills, the terrain was more difficult. J.B. trusted a horse's senses more than his own, and he rode with a slack rein, letting the blue-roan pick its way. Moonlight revealed a narrow cattle trail out in the open, but down in the shadows of the ravines only the horse could see the trail. J.B. had lived on horseback since he was a boy, and he sat easily, relaxed, even when the horse scrambled up rocky rises and slid down embankments. He knew the blue-roan well enough to know that the horse didn't want to fall any more than he wanted it to.

They traveled out of a deep ravine, through acres of buck brush, and came out onto a wide vega. The ranch buildings sat back against a high ridge that rose out of the ground to the north. A wagon road, leading from the buildings toward El Rey, was plainly visible, and so was the huge CC painted on the side of a barn. It wasn't long until daylight. A rooster crowed, and a cow lowed somewhere nearby.

J.B. picked out the white two-story house and saw a dim light in a front window. He spotted a low building, a bunk house, and noticed with satisfaction that it was dark. Another, smaller house, also dark, sat fifty feet west of the big house.

She should have been expecting him. After all, she'd asked him to come here. But she had expected him many hours earlier, and had probably given up and gone to bed. He hoped he could awaken her without stirring anybody else.

The horse's hooves made little sound as he rode up to the main house, but it was enough to excite a dog, which instantly alerted the one man in the bunkhouse. J.B. had an urge to turn the horse around and run, but he reminded himself again that the girl had asked him to come. The best thing to do, he decided, was to stand still until she came out.

A tall, square-jawed young cowboy ran out of the bunkhouse buttoning his pants as he ran. He was bare-headed and his shirttail was flapping in the breeze. He carried a pistol awkwardly while he buttoned his pants.

J.B. stayed on his horse.

"Who are you?" the cowboy yelled. He recognized J.B. then, and said, "Why, you're the...you're the feller that..."

"Yeah," J.B. said, "that's me."

"What're you doin' here?"

"Miss Crandall asked me to come."

The front door of the house opened and she came out, fully dressed but with her hair tousled. She ran her fingers through her tawny, shoulder-length hair and stopped in front of J.B. and his horse. Frown wrinkles appeared between her eyes. She stared at him a moment—then started talking.

"Where in the blue-eyed world have you been, you couldn't have gotten lost, even a dumb cowhand can follow a creek, and I've been waiting for you for hours, well don't just sit there like a wooden Indian, get down and come on in the house."

He followed her up the walk, wiped his boots carefully on a sisal mat, removed his hat, and stepped shyly into the room. The room was furnished with hand-carved oak furniture that held thick cushions. The floor was mostly covered with a thick rug containing a floral pattern, and the walls were covered with wallpaper containing another floral design. The part of the floor not covered was also of oak and polished to a shine.

But the room was in disarray. Wooden crates and large cardboard packing boxes were stacked on one side. The walls were bare of pictures and the furniture was bare of knickknacks of the kind that J.B. had expected to find in a well-to-do family's house.

It was the first time he had ever been inside a big house, and he couldn't help staring at his surroundings, at how ranch owners and their families lived. Even in disarray, the room was in no way comparable to the bare wooden floors and homemade furniture he grew up with and had lived with in the bunkhouses.

She motioned him to a big chair with thick, soft cushions, but he bypassed it and sat on a footstool.

"Anyway, I'm glad you finally showed up. I was afraid you decided to leave the country, and I was afraid that if you did, the mystery of my uncle's disappearance would never be cleared up."

J.B. was still too dumbfounded by his surroundings to speak.

"I know," she went on, "that Sheriff White would pin the whole thing on you, and the real culprit, whoever he might be, would go free." She was looking intently at him. "I didn't miss my guess, did I? You really are innocent? Speak to me."

"Huh, uh, yes, ma'am. I didn't hurt nobody. I was in Santa Fe the day your uncle disappeared."

He stared at his boots a moment, then looked up. "Uh, Miss Crandall, how did you know? I mean, how did you know I didn't have anything to do with it? Why did you help me break jail?"

Her answer was slow in coming, and she spoke carefully. "Well, you see, J.B., my uncle is a little, uh, eccentric. He has worked very hard all his life and he has suffered many disappointments. He was married, briefly, but his wife was more interested in drinking and partying than in making a home. She left him without saying good-bye. And his brother and sister-in-law, that is, my father and mother, were killed by raiding Apaches three years ago."

She paused, and J.B. wondered if she would get around to answering his question. He said, "I've heard about the 'Paches gettin' out of their reservation and killin' folks. I never blamed 'em much for breakin' out, but the people they kill're ones that never had nothin' to do with their troubles."

If she heard him, she didn't let on. She continued, "Uncle Len has been fortunate, economically speaking, but he seemed to remember only his misfortunes. It seemed to, well, eat on him. He was feeling bad. This ranch belonged to him and my father as partners, and now I own—owned—a half interest. Uncle Len blamed all women for the way his wife treated him, never mind that his brother's wife, my mother, worked as hard as he did and was always loyal. He became a woman hater. He sent me off to school to get rid of me. When I dropped out of the university after three years and came back here, he seemed to get more unhappy."

Miss Crandall had been looking at the floor as she talked, but now she leveled her gaze at J.B. "What I'm getting at is, I don't know that anything bad happened to Uncle Len. He once talked of selling the ranch and moving to Denver. He could have taken his hoard, lied about going to the bank with it, and ridden north. I couldn't let someone hang for a murder that might not have happened.

"And I suspected you were innocent the first time I saw you. It was your anger, your outrage at being locked up in jail. A guilty man would have been more worried than angry. And the way you tore into John Buetel. You didn't know it, but you gave my morale a boost when you made a fool of him."

Silence followed. Then J.B. asked, "Why was your uncle carrying so much money?"

"That was one of his eccentricities. He didn't trust banks—

though he didn't mind borrowing money from them. He kept his money hidden in this house. We—he—shipped nine carloads of fat beeves up to Denver a week ago, and he insisted on being paid in cash."

"Did he always carry it with him?"

"Oh, no. Let me back up a moment. As I said, he borrowed money from the bank to buy more land and add to the ranch holdings here. Well, that gave the bank a mortgage on the ranch, and the mortgage was due. Uncle Len was taking the money to the bank to pay off the mortgage."

J.B. nodded. "Uh huh. And that is why—I'm almost afraid to ask—why you said you 'owned' a half interest in this ranch, instead of 'own' a half interest?"

She nodded. "That's it exactly. The deadline was the day Uncle Len disappeared. As of this morning, the Piñon Valley National Bank owns and operates the CC Ranch, all the livestock, equipment, buildings, this house, and even the furnishings in this house." She pointed to the packing boxes. "All I get to keep are the personal items."

"Are you sure about that? Could your uncle have miscounted or anything?"

"No doubt about it. When I came home from the university, I took over the bookkeeping. That was my major subject at the university. And there is no doubt about it. I expect John Buetel here anytime now to take possession."

J.B.'s eyebrows went up. "That the same Buetel I tangled with back at the livery stable?"

"He's the president and chairman of the board of the bank." That impish smile played around the corners of her mouth again. "He's a big shot, but I'll bet he's got a sore behind."

The cowboy grinned too, but his grin was short-lived. "Now he's mad at you too for helpin' me."

"It doesn't matter. He didn't like me anyway. Last week I made him go over every word, every figure, in the mortgage contract, and he didn't appreciate that. Said something about how women ought to be baking bread and raising kids instead of running a ranch.

"And," she continued, "he and Uncle Len hated each other.

Uncle Len never passed up a chance to irritate him. Those longhorn beeves you saw in the railroad pens belong to the Box 0, which belongs to John Buetel. They moved the cattle there to ship them to the packing house, but the railroad couldn't find enough cattle cars, and they are having to keep them in the pens and feed them hay. CC Ranch hay. We had the only hay for sale in this end of the county, and Uncle Len made John Buetel pay dearly for it."

J.B. considered telling her about those cattle and the stampede he had caused, but he decided against it. Telling her would serve no purpose, he decided. He didn't know what to say next. He stood up, shuffled his feet, twisted the brim of his black hat, sat back down.

"I'm sure sorry, Miss Crandall. I guess I thought only hired men could have bad luck. You've sure got more than your share. Uh, if there's anything I can do to help." He shrugged.

"As a matter of fact, there is," she said, holding his gaze. "I want to find out what happened to Uncle Len. If he left the country, I want to know it, and if he is the victim of foul play, I want to know that, too. I need help. I have no money now to pay anyone, and I thought that since you are, uh, footloose and all—"

"Sure," he interjected. "You bet I'll help you. Anyway I can. You saved my life."

A knock on the door interrupted their conversation. "It can't be that banker, not this early," she said as she went to the door and opened it.

When the door was opened, J.B. noticed it was daylight outside. The tall, young cowboy stood there with his hat in his hands and a shy look on his face.

"Why, Joel," said Miss Crandall. "Come in."

He stepped through the door. "I came to help you move, Miss Crandall. I can hitch up the team of sorrels to the spring wagon and carry your stuff to town for you if you want."

"Aren't you afraid of losing your job here, Joel?"

For a moment the shyness passed and he asserted himself. "Hang the job. Your family has been good to me, Miss Crandall. If you want, I'll help you move."

Her eyes and voice softened. "Thank you, Joel, but you don't really want to lose your job. Mr. Buetel said he intended to promote you to foreman. After all, you've been here longer than the other men and you know the country. And you stayed after the other men left."

His face reddened. "You have to get your stuff to town, Miss Crandall."

"I'll manage, Joel. And just think about it. As foreman you can move into the foreman's house, and it will be a nice home for you and your future bride. Uncle Len and I intended to fix it up for you. I was very happy to learn that you're going to marry that nice girl at Winters' Cafe. She'll be a lovely wife. I can't let you risk that, Joel."

"I'm gonna do it for you, Miss Crandall." He turned to leave. "I'll harness the team right now, before Mr. Buetel gets here."

"Thank you, Joel, but please don't. Not without Mr. Buetel's permission."

He opened the door and looked back. "I'm gonna do it." He left.

"He wants to be loyal," J.B. said.

"Yes, he's loyal and honest. But there has been something lacking in him. I don't know. I guess it's because he came from a poor family and has always had to look up to people like me. He's easily cowed." She frowned thoughtfully. "He surprised me just now. He really surprised me."

J.B. stood up. "That's better'n bein' a bully. And as big as he is, he could be a bully if he wanted to."

"Yes," she said, "he has his qualities."

J.B. walked to the door and stood before it. "What do you want me to do, Miss Crandall? Just name it."

"First thing," she answered, "is vacate this house. And next, I guess, is ride north, to Raton. If Uncle Len headed for Denver he would have stopped in Raton, and someone would have seen him."

"What'll you do if you find out he went through Raton and was safe and headed for Denver?"

She answered hesitantly. "I don't know. The money he is carrying is half mine. My dad—his brother—was a partner in this ranch, and as my dad's heir, I'm entitled to half the proceeds. But"— she shrugged, then sighed—"half the money won't pay off the note, and I don't know... If Uncle Len wanted it that badly...I don't know."

It occurred to J.B. that she was showing a different personality now. No longer the headstrong, take-charge type, she was now unsure of herself and asking for help. She was afraid to look for her missing uncle alone. She needed a man to lean on. Somehow, that pleased him.

"So what you want to do, Miss Crandall, is ride up to Raton and see if your uncle passed through there?"

"Yes, I guess that would be the best thing to do." She talked on, as if to herself. "I could take a stage to Denver, find him, and get my share of the money. I would have no trouble finding a job and earning a living as an accountant."

She turned her attention to J.B. again. "I'll have to decide what to do next when we get there."

"And," the cowboy asked, "what if we don't find no sign of him?"

"Then we'll have to do a lot of riding. We'll have to search this entire end of the county. If he didn't go through Raton, then he has definitely been murdered and robbed."

"Okay," J.B. shrugged, "but I've got a small problem. It'll take all day to get to Raton, and by that time my horse will've had a saddle on his back for almost twenty-four hours, and he hasn't had much feed or rest. I sure could use a fresh mount."

"We'll take two good horses from the remuda. Under terms of the mortgage, I'm entitled to absolutely nothing here, but I'm going to take two horses anyway. Just let ol' Buetel try to make something of it." Her jaw tightened. "Just let him try."

Now she was the determined, scrappy woman J.B. first saw, and that pleased him too. But it occurred to him that taking two horses might be considered stealing. She could get by with it under the circumstances—the local lawmen would excuse her conduct—but if he was caught with a stolen horse, he would be in serious trouble. He had no friends anywhere in the vicinity of El Rey, that was for certain. Riding along with this girl could cost him his freedom for a long, long time. Even his life. But—well, hell, he was in trouble anyway and this girl had helped him.

"I hate to take a horse that might belong to somebody else," he said, "but if I'm goin' anywhere, I've got no choice. I cain't ask Ol' Amigo to carry me much farther without a couple day's rest and some good feed."

"We'll turn him out just below the hay meadow," she said. "The grass is good, and you can catch him again in a few days." She looked down at herself. "Now, I need to take one change of clothes, which I can wrap up in my rain slicker, and something to eat."

CHAPTER 5

She left the room and hurried upstairs. When she came down, she was carrying a rolled slicker. Once outside the house, she hollered for Joel, and the tall cowboy came at a dogtrot from the barn.

"Have you wrangled in the horses yet? I need two good mounts. How about old Champagne and that tall buckskin? High Pockets, I believe you call him."

"Yes, ma'am," he said, "but," he looked at J.B. and back at the girl, "are you, uh..."

"Just run in the remuda, Joel," she said firmly.

"Yes, ma'am, I already done that."

J.B. looked over his head and saw fifteen or twenty horses milling inside a corral. He walked back to the house and the hitchrail, untied the blue-roan, led it back to the corrals, and pulled off the saddle. "I lost my rope," he said to the girl. "Can I borrow somethin' to lead him with?"

"We'll find something," she said.

Joel roped out the two horses for them. He stood in the center of the corral and swung his loop overhand in one smooth motion so that it sailed out, turned over in the air, and dropped around the head of the horse he wanted. It was a way of catching a horse on the far side of the corral with other horses between it and the roper. J.B. smiled at the pleasure of watching a good roper in action.

They went into the kitchen, and J.B. and Joel sat with little to say to each other while Miss Crandall fried eggs and pan-fried some steaks in smoking hot fat. They ate in silence, as cowboys do. J.B. once glanced at Joel and caught the tall cowboy glancing at him. He detected suspicion, and he also detected a warning that he had better not mistreat Miss Crandall. He tried to think of the words to tell the cowboy that he had no intention of mistreating anybody, especially Miss Crandall, but he said nothing.

The sun had just shown itself on the eastern horizon when J.B. and the girl rode out. She was dressed in freshly laundered Levi's and a blue checked shirt. The Levi's had a crease down the front, and J.B. knew it took a lot of starch and a lot of work with a hot iron on a flat board to develop that crease. This time she let her tawny hair hang down to her shoulders under the hat.

The buckskin was a fine horse. It had a good mouth and it reacted properly to only a flick of the reins. It was a good traveler, although not as good as the blue-roan. They rode north at a slow, easy trot, and the girl remarked that it was always good to be on horseback on a beautiful high-country morning. Her cheerfulness was surprising to J.B., and he said so.

"How can anybody who has just lost a good ranch be so happy?" he asked.

"It's my nature. I'm a happy person. My dad was the same way. The harder times got, the happier he was. And as I said back at the house, I've got a good education and I can earn a living anywhere."

They rode in silence for a time. The girl's eyes were busy taking in the scenery: the rocky ravines, the stunted piñons, the yucca, now in bloom with bell-shaped pods, the tall bunch grass, the jagged mountains to the west. Twice she took a long look behind her, and J.B. had the feeling that she was taking a look at something she feared she might never see again. When she spoke, she spoke almost inaudibly, as if to herself. "I was born and raised on that ranch. I'm going to miss it terribly."

J.B. tried to think of something to say that would make her feel better, but he could think of nothing. They rode on, keeping a northerly course with the mountains to their left. Finally, she glanced at J.B. and smiled a weak smile.

"If Uncle Len went to Denver, perhaps that's where I'll go. If I find him I'll try to get my share of the money, and if I don't, well, as I said, I can make a living. I might even enjoy the big city. Yes, I'll make myself enjoy it."

She was forcing herself to think cheerful thoughts, J.B. knew. But if her mood wasn't glum, his was, out of pity for her, and he looked away.

"Tell me, J.B.," she said brightly, "why do you call yourself by your initials? What is your full name, if you don't mind my asking?"

"It's, uh, it's..."

"I see. Never mind. It's really none of my business." He knew she was trying to make conversation to keep her mind off her loss, and he knew he would be an *estupido* if he didn't go along with it.

"Well, it's, uh, it's Julian."

"Julian?"

That smile was beginning at the corners of her mouth again. He was happy that he could make her smile.

"Yeah, Julian. But nobody calls me that 'less they're a lot bigger'n I am."

Her smile widened. "What does the B stand for?"

"Bartholomew."

The smile turned to laughter. "You're joshing. Julian Bartholomew?"

"Julian Bartholomew Watts."

"Well, excuse me for laughing, but that's the funniest name I ever heard. Why did your folks give you a handle like that?"

Normally, J.B. saw red when anyone made fun of his name, but now, for her sake, he decided to go along with the joke. "I was the last born of three boys, and they figured if they gave me an unusual name maybe I'd turn out to be an unusual man."

"What did they call you for short," she laughed, "Jul—"

He cut her off abruptly. "Don't say it." He was laughing with her, but he made it clear he was serious, too. "Don't you dare say it. I've been in fist fights over that since I was a kid."

"With a name like that, a boy would have to learn to fight—or play with the girls." They were riding side by side on a wagon road and she studied his face, still smiling. "And you don't strike me as the kind that would run from a fight."

They traveled on, keeping to the yucca flats and skirting the high mountain ridges to the west of them. Off to the east J.B. saw a creek meandering along parallel to the wagon road they were following, and far ahead he could see a groove of cottonwoods that were irrigated by the creek. At midday they stopped, loosened their cinches, and while the horses grazed, they ate roast beef between thick slices of bread. They drank from the creek, and when the girl flattened out on her stomach and put her lips to the water, her denim pants were pulled tight in places, and J.B. wondered how he had ever mistaken her for a boy. Gaw-nd, he thought to himself, that's what makes dogs run around.

Storm clouds gathered over the mountains shortly after they tightened their cinches and rode on. She said it was the time of year when a shower broke out almost every night in the high country. The showers were what made the land around there so good for grazing, she said. She went on to explain that rainwater picks up certain chemicals as it falls through the sky and that is better for making things grow than the creek water used for irrigation. "That's one of the things I learned at the university," she said. "But I think every cowman in the West knows that without going to college." It was about that time that J.B. noticed they were being followed.

He had caught only a glimpse of them when they topped a rise, but he knew there were three men and they were overtaking him and the girl. "Miss Crandall," he said, trying to find a hole in her conversation so he could tell her about it, "we, uh, are about to have some company."

She glanced back, but felt no alarm. "Call me Shine," she said. "That's been my nickname stance I was a towheaded child, and since we're traveling partners..."

But he was worried. "Uh, Shine, I don't know if it means anything or not, but they are about to catch up with us. Could it be ol' Buetel sent his hired gunsels after us because we took these horses?"

She took another look. "I don't know. It could be they just happen to be going the same place we're going, but they do seem to be in a hurry."

"Let's git off the road and see if they follow us."

They hadn't gone more than a hundred yards at a right angle to the road when J.B. knew they were in for a bad time. The three men cut across the yucca and prickly pear and headed toward them."

"Do you know any of 'em?" J.B. asked.

The three men were riding at a full gallop now, and she watched them come closer. "Yes," she said finally. "They're Buetel's men. I recognize the man with the derby hat. And the horses. They're CC horses."

"Him? I recognize him too. He was one of the mob that wanted to hang me."

She pulled her hat brim down to shade her eyes. "I don't see the sheriff or any of his deputies among them. Only they can make an arrest."

"Listen," J.B. said, "that whole town's after me now. We'd better ride. We can outrun 'em. Their horses are winded."

"No," she said. "I'll not run from John Buetel or any of his hired hooligans. The Crandall family still has some influence around here."

"Yeah, but I've got no influence, and those fellers're packin' shootin' irons."

"Don't run," she said, stopping her horse. "They wouldn't dare bother me or anyone with me."

As the three riders approached at a gallop, two of them drew pistols. Derby Hat was in the lead. They were all armed with pistols and rifles.

"Caught you, didn't we," Derby Hat said to J.B. He glanced at the girl and back at him. "She ain't gonna help you this time."

They surrounded the two, their horses blowing from the run. Besides Derby Hat there were two more men J.B. remembered seeing through the window of his jail cell. One of them wore a neatly trimmed moustache, flat-brimmed hat, long black coat, black gloves, and a pearl-handled six-gun on each hip. He looked to J.B. like a carbon copy of professional gamblers he had seen in cowtowns, mining towns, and railroad towns all over the southwest. And J.B. would have bet that those six-guns, tied low for a quick draw, allowed him to cheat and get by with it. He was the one who spoke next.

"This the galoot that stampeded them cattle?"

"That's him," said Derby Hat.

The man raised his six-gun so that J.B. was looking down the bore. "I oughta put a slug in 'im. I ain't found my horse yet."

"Stop that," said Miss Crandall. "What do you think you're doing? Put those guns away."

Derby Hat stared at her a moment, then, "You ain't tellin' me what to do, lady. This saddle bum killed a man for his money and come near to wipin' out a town just for meanness. He ain't gettin' away this time. Git off that hoss," he said to J.B.

J.B. hesitated, and the third man drew his six-shooter. He looked to be a working cowhand, with the name "Ed" painted on his batwing chaps. "If anybody's gonna shoot 'im, it's gonna be me. He owes me a team of horses and a buckboard."

"We'll never get any money out of this *como se llama*," the gambler said. "These saddle tramps spend all their bucks drinkin' and whorin'. When you see 'em ridin' it's because they're broke."

"Only thing I can't figure out," Ed put in, "is why this purty lil' girl is ridin' with 'im."

"I asked him to ride with me," she said. "I don't like to travel alone, and he's a man I can trust. Not like you hoodlums."

Ed took his lass rope off his saddle, built a loop, and pitched it overhand around J.B.'s shoulders. "The man said git down," he growled, "so git down 'fore I jerk you down."

J.B. dismounted, feeling totally helpless afoot, with three guns aimed at him and no weapon of his own.

In two quick movements, the girl spurred her horse up beside J.B. and reached down and lifted the loop from his shoulders. She faced the three men with fire in her eyes. "Now you men git. Sheriff White will tan your hides when he hears about this. The Crandall family still has friends."

Derby Hat holstered his gun, dismounted, and grabbed her reins just below the bridle bit, which gave him control of her horse. "You Crandalls're all crazy, and you're settin' on a stolen hoss, and we got the right to arrest you."

"By what authority?"

"By Mr. Buetel's authority. He sent us after you. You're both guilty of hoss theft. Now, you git off your hoss too." He grabbed her by the arm and pulled her roughly from the saddle.

J.B. hit him. His right hand blow split Derby Hat's lower lip, and a quick left hand knocked him down. "Where I come from you don't treat a lady like that," he growled.

The fight was short-lived. The other two riders quickly dismounted, a blow from behind knocked the slightly built cowboy to his knees. Three pairs of rough hands held him face down in the dirt, yanked his arms behind him, and tied his hands. J.B. tried to fight, but it was useless under three bigger men. He could hear the girl screaming at them, "Let him go. Get off him, you hoodlums." When J.B.'s hands were tied painfully tight, he was hauled to his feet. Derby Hat hit him in the face with a hard fist. J.B. staggered back but stayed right side up.

Then Derby Hat was under attack. The girl flew into him, both fists flailing and both feet kicking. "You coward," she yelled. "Hit a man while he's tied, will you."

At least two of her blows found their target, and Derby Hat, who already had a split lip, suffered more bruises. But that fight too was short-lived. A heavy-handed blow caught her upside the face and sent her sprawling. The blow knocked her hat off and her blond hair fell across her face. She was immediately on her feet again, and again was kicking and clawing at Derby Hat. It took two big men to pull her off and hold her back. J.B. struggled against his bonds, but could do nothing.

One of the men had to chuckle. "I allus said I'd rather tangle with a catymount than a woman."

Derby Hat dragged a shirt sleeve across his mouth and cursed. "You goddam little bitch. I oughta..." His eyes took in the beauty of her then, with her blond hair in her face and her blue eyes shooting sparks. His eyes roved from her hair downward, and his voice dropped an octave, "I oughta, I oughta make you..." He was thinking it, but he was afraid to say it.

"Mebbe we ought to turn her loose," said Ed. "Mebbe she does have friends."

Derby Hat was too busy undressing her with his eyes to answer for a moment. Finally, he said, "No, I got an idea. Tie her up too."

"You ain't gonna...?" someone asked.

Derby Hat relaxed, a slow smile forming on his face. "Naw. Not now. I got another idea. It came to me when I heard these two was

56

ridin' together."

"What's that, Dutch?"

"Money, that's what's that. Two saddlebags of money ol' Crazy Len was carryin' when he left the CC Ranch. Either these two killed 'im and hid the money, or he's still alive and they know where he is— and where that money is."

Miss Crandall had ceased struggling, but she still had fire in her eyes. "That's absurd."

"It ain't absurd," Derby Hat, better known as Dutch, mimicked her word. "It makes sense to me." He untied the slicker behind her saddle and shook it out. A dress and a pair of women's shoes fell out.

"She ain't got it and he ain't got it but I'll bet they know where it is." He frowned, thinking. "I suspicioned all along when I heard Old Len was missin'. He didn't like her and she didn't like him, and she fixed it up with this saddle tramp to get his money."

The three men thought that over. Derby Hat continued, "That money's probly stashed somewhere between here and Raton where they can git at it and head for the big city. Yessir, they was headin' for a high ol' time on that money."

"Let's git it from 'em." It was the gambler talking. Derby Hat turned to face the girl. "Where is it?"

She spat at him. "You're so stupid you don't know anything about the Crandall family, and I don't know where the money is, and I wouldn't tell you if I did."

Turning next to J.B., Derby Hat pulled his pistol, cocked the hammer back, and placed the end of the barrel against the cowboy's forehead. "You'll tell. Tell us or I'll spill your brains all over this county."

J.B. was scared. But he was also angry. He had heard all he wanted to hear about money, seen all he wanted to see of these men, and was damned tired of having guns pointed at him. "Go choke yourself."

The finger on the trigger tightened, and the cowboy's heart jumped into his throat. He saw death coming, and he let out an involuntary gasp.

"Wait." It was the gambler. "He won't tell us anything if he's dead. There's ways to make men talk."

The trigger finger relaxed. "I can kill 'im and get the information out of her, but maybe this ain't the place to do it."

"Right, and I know a cabin up on the rim where nobody's lived since last fall. We got all the time in the world, and up there nobody's gonna come along and see what's happenin'"

Derby Hat took a long look around. "There ain't much traffic on this road, but maybe we'd better git up in them hills. Git 'em on their hosses."

Derby Hat borrowed a pigging string—the kind used to tie cattle down—from the man named Ed in the batwing chaps and approached the girl. "Now do you wanta put your hands behind your back like a nice little gal or do I have to rassle with you?"

When he reached for her, she gave him a painful kick on the shin with her hard-heeled boots and went for his face with a clawed hand at the same time. Her nails left a red streak on his left cheek.

He was in pain but not handicapped, and he grabbed her wrists in both of his big hands, tripped her by putting one foot behind her right foot, and fell to the ground on top of her.

J.B. screamed, "Let her go, you sonofabitch, or by God I'll—"

All he got for his effort was a thump on top of the head. Derby Hat had her two wrists in one hand now, and he groped for her breast with the other. He was grinning with pleasure.

With a hard desperate twisting jump, J.B. broke free, and in two more long steps he was close enough to kick him on the shoulder, knocking him aside. Again, J.B. was hit on the head and jerked to the ground.

Miss Crandall jumped up, but two men pulled her down again, turned her over on her stomach, and tied her hands behind her back. Then she was picked up bodily and placed in her saddle. Derby Hat wiped a hand across his scratched cheek, got on his horse, and took the reins to her horse. J.B. was forced onto his horse, and his horse was led by the gambler.

It was the second time in the past few days that he was helpless on a horse controlled by someone else, and the rage within him was almost more than lie could stand. All he wanted right then was a good, hard kick at that sonofabitch in the Derby Hat. Hell, he'd gladly take a dozen punches just to get one punch at him.

He fumed and sputtered, but could do nothing. And slowly, as he realized that the girl was not hurt, the rage subsided and he began to think. He remembered how it felt to have a gun bore pressed against his forehead and a finger tightening on the trigger. Another fraction of an inch and the top of his head would be lying back there in the dirt. His luck wasn't all bad. He was lucky to be alive. The problem now, he thought, was how to stay alive.

Hell, he couldn't tell them anything about any money, because he didn't know anything. They only thought he knew. Seemed a lot of folks were convinced he knew where two saddlebags of money were hidden, and where the body of a man named Len Crandall was. Hell, he never saw the man. They only thought he had.

That brought an idea to his mind. He mulled it over. What he was thinking wasn't the gutsiest thing to do, but it might work. It might save their lives. It would at least buy them some time, and with enough time, something might happen in their favor. His plan wasn't perfect, but it was the best he could think of.

CHAPTER 6

Both J.B. and the girl were bareheaded. Their hats had been knocked off in the struggles and they had not had a chance to put them back on. His reddish-blond hair stuck out in all directions, and her blond hair hung over her face and sometimes in her eyes.

They entered a steep canyon and followed a dim game trail. At one point the trail was blocked by a rockslide, and they had to turn the five horses around and go back a hundred yards and cross a swift creek at a lower point. Conversation was light. The gambler led the way. He said he knew of the cabin because he and a hunting companion once spent the night up there. He believed it had been built by a trapper, and was a wreck but that it at least had a roof.

The horses climbed, scrambled over rocks, slid down banks, and climbed some more. The canyon walls were high, steep enough to block the sun, and the five riders were in the cool shadows most of the time. The girl shivered, and J.B. felt sorry for her again. He wished he could do something—put a coat around her, brush her hair from her eyes, anything. He silently swore at their predicament.

Derby Hat said he was glad they had been able to pick up some fresh horses at the CC Ranch, and the man in the batwing chaps said they were all lucky that a friend of his had ridden into El Rey after the stampede that night and could use his horse to catch some of the others. "We'd've been afoot for a long time if he hadn't 'a came along," he said.

The gambler looked back at J.B. and said, "Nobody'll blame us if we bury this *Tejano*." He chuckled. "The only thing they'll blame us for is not bringin' him back to town for a public hangin'."

J.B. was turning thoughts and ideas over in his mind and wasn't paying much attention to the conversation. Then Derby Hat said something that grabbed his attention and stuck in his mind.

"Mr. Buetel sure wanted this cowboy hung. He was disappointed then, but we won't disappoint 'im this time."

No one added to that comment, and the group rode on in silence.

It was only an hour's ride but it was sundown when they rode out of the upper end of the canyon and found themselves on the edge of a wide, pine-studded valley. A few cows with freshly-branded calves grazed near a one-room log cabin, and a buck deer with a wide rack of antlers bounded into the timber ahead.

The man with "Ed" painted on his batwing chaps nodded toward the calves and commented as how the Diamond A riders had worked that part of the country not long ago, but there wouldn't be anyone around now.

The cabin was vacant, all right. In fact, it hadn't been lived in for years. It was made of logs dragged down from the timbered hills, but the logs had not been peeled, and were rotting. The roof was caved in over one corner and the door had long ago been torn off its strap hinges. Ed guessed a bear had torn the door down. "Best thing to do in bear country," he said, "is just leave the door open."

"Or," the gambler put in, "don't leave anything that smells like grub inside."

An old pole corral with most of the poles down stood nearby, and a creek ran behind the corral and the cabin and on across the valley.

They dismounted in front of the cabin. J.B. was jerked down off his horse and landed on his left shoulder, but the girl was handled more gently. Next came a conversation about whether to try to force information out of the captives now or wait until daylight. Derby Hat was impatient.

"Why wait?" he asked. "Nobody but us'll ever know what's gonna happen up here."

"We got all the time in the world," the gambler said. "That's why we came this far. This *Tejano* is stubborn, I can see that, and we'll have to do more than point a gun at 'im to make 'im talk."

"Well," said Ed, "I know all you fellers've slept on a saddle blanket and missed a couple of meals before. If we find that money, it'll be worth it."

Derby Hat shrugged. "All right, let's build a fire and at least keep from freezin'."

"What'll we do with the horses?" the gambler asked.

"Tie 'em to them old corral posts," Derby Hat said. "If we can miss supper, them brutes can miss supper too."

A fire was built and horses were unsaddled. J.B. winced when he saw the treatment given his custom-made saddle. Derby Hat dumped it upside down and said how the thick wool skirt liner would make a tolerable pillow. The cowboy hated to see the skirts and seat jockeys bent out of shape, even if they could be repaired in time.

Three of the saddle blankets were Navaho, made of angora wool. They were doubled and used under saddles. Now, they were spread around the fire as thin pallets.

J.B. and the girl were quiet while camp was made, and then they were ordered to sit on the ground, their hands still tied behind their backs. The cowboy cast a look at the girl and she looked back at him, expressionless. By the time camp was made, it was dark.

"All right," Derby Hat said as the fire cast flickering light over the group. He stood in front of the captives, feet apart, thumbs hooked inside his red suspenders. "I ain't waitin'. I can take this lil' lady inside that cabin and get all kinds of information out of her." He grinned wickedly.

"She'll prob'ly talk the fastest," said the gambler, "but I've got a score to settle with this cowboy." Without another word, he picked a burning stick out of the fire, walked over to J.B., and stuck it in his face.

J.B. jerked back, trying to escape the flame. The gambler shoved it in his face again. The cowboy's hair caught fire briefly, and J.B. flopped over onto his stomach, rubbing his head in the dirt. The fire went out.

Miss Crandall screamed, "Stop it. Stop it."

A chuckle came from the gambler. He dropped the stick into the fire, grabbed J.B. by the hair, and pulled him to his knees. "Want some more, killer?"

J.B.'s eyebrows were singed and a hot pain flared in his left cheek. Now is the time to say it, he thought. Say it now. Don't let him do that again. He opened his mouth to speak, but no words came out.

The girl was moaning, "Please don't. We don't know where the money is. Please don't hurt him."

The gambler backed off, scowling. Derby Hat took over.

He pushed J.B. onto his back, and pulled off one of his boots, then the sock. "Hold 'im," he said to the men. The gambler and Ed jumped astraddle the cowboy's body and held him so tightly he could barely squirm. "This'll make most men sing like a warbler," Derby Hat said, as he grabbed another burning stick from the fire. J.B. clinched his teeth and tried to hold it back, but a groan escaped him as his left foot was singed. The girl screamed again, her eyes wide with horror. "Stop it. Please stop it."

"Shut her up," said Derby Hat.

The gambler left his perch astraddle J.B., got behind the girl, and clamped a hand over her mouth. She bit his fingers. He swore, grabbed her by the hair, and jerked her over backwards. "Lady or no lady," he muttered, "I oughta scalp you and blame it on the Indians."

Derby Hat watched what was happening to the girl and chuckled. "My ol' pop aways said when a woman puts herself in a man's place, she oughta be treated like a man." His smile faded and he shook his head sadly. "But man, that one is all woman. Man, I'd like to..."

The gambler was impatient. He stood up, leaving the girl on the ground. "Come on, let's finish this job." He jumped astraddle J.B. again, pinning him down.

Pain went through J.B.'s foot again, and again a moan escaped him.

"All right, let 'im set up." The weight was lifted from J.B. He sat up. He looked at his foot, expecting to see nothing but cooked flesh. He was surprised to see only an abnormal redness. But gawd, how it burned.

Derby Hat squatted in front of him. "Where is it?" Now is the time, J.B. thought. Why let them burn him again. Say it now. He opened his mouth, and again nothing came out.

"Now it's her turn." Derby Hat stood up, grabbed the girl by the hair, and lifted her to her feet. Holding her by the hair with one hand, he ripped open her blue checked shirt with the other.

Her white underclothes showed inside the shirt.

Derby Hat shot a glance at the other men, licked his lips with pleasure, and fumbled with her belt buckle. Miss Crandall stood stony-faced, saying nothing. They all waited, breathing shallowly, as Derby Hat undid the top button on her Levi's.

It was J.B. who broke the silence. "Don't hurt her. I'll tell you."

The other two men immediately forgot the girl and turned their attention to J.B. Derby Hat turned his head toward J.B., and the girl twisted away from him. He grabbed her again, but the gambler barked, "Forget her, will you. We're about to get rich."

J.B. had it planned. He remembered seeing a grove of cottonwoods a half mile farther up the wagon road to Raton, and he used his imagination to picture a rocky outcropping a hundred yards or so to the east of the cottonwoods. He could imagine a crevice in the outcropping large enough to hold a pair of saddlebags.

He told them about it. "I hid the old man's body and his saddle in a 'royo back near El Rey," he said, "and turned the horse loose,"

Once he started talking, the words came easily. J.B. had always had an active imagination, and he almost made himself believe what he was saying. "It was just luck. I saw the old man on the road to El Rey, stopped and palavered a while. I suspicioned he had somethin' in those saddlebags by the way he acted, you know, like he was afraid of me. I put my forty-five on 'im and had a look. When I saw all that money, I shot 'im. I knew there would be a big hunt on for 'im and anyone with money to spend would be suspicious., so I figured I'd go back to El Rey, git a job cowboyin' on the Diamond A, then pick up the money next fall and head for the bright lights someplace."

While he talked, a full moon appeared on top of the eastern horizon, and J.B. could see the pleased expression on their faces.

"Well, I'll be damned," said the gambler. "That's just what I figured."

"If it hadn't been for us," said Ed, "he'd've got away with it."

He and the gambler picked up their saddles and carried them

toward the horses. "I know where them cottonwoods are," the gambler said over his shoulder.

"If this backshooter is tellin' the truth, we'll all be rich before sunup," said Ed.

Derby Hat watched them but made no move to join them. "We can't all go," he said. "Someone has to stay here and keep an eye on 'em. 'Case he's lyin'."

"You're not goin' with us?" the gambler asked as he cinched a saddle on his horse.

"No," Derby Hat said. "If you don't find no money, you come back here and we'll spread-eagle 'im and burn 'im up a piece at a time." He looked at J.B. "You'll beg us to kill you."

He turned to the other men and spoke sharply. "But if you fellers don't come back, I'll know where to find you. I'll shoot first and ask questions later."

The gambler reined his horse toward the canyon and said over his shoulder, "We'll be back. It'll be a mite tricky ridin' down in the dark, but that moon'll help some." Ed followed him.

When they were gone, Derby Hat put more wood on the fire and stood for a long moment with his head down, thinking. As if he had reached a decision, he went to the horses and slipped the bridles off the two that J.B. and the girl had ridden. Happy to be free, the two horses left on the run. The one horse still tied danced around on the end of the reins, wanting to join them.

"You ain't gonna need 'em," Derby Hat said when he walked back to the fire. The girl had sat down again, her white underclothes still showing in her open shirt. Derby Hat stood in front of her.

"Now it's your turn, Miss godamighty Crandall." A cruel smile twisted his face. "You know where that money is, and you're gonna tell ol' Dutch all about it, ain't you."

"I just told you," J.B. said.

"Shut up," he snapped without taking his eyes off the girl. "Now ol' Dutch can be mighty good to a purty lil' gal like you, or ol' Dutch can be mean." He took her by the hair and pulled her to her feet again. "Which do you want?"

Her shoulders slumped. "All right," she mumbled. "I'll tell you where it is."

As she spoke, a cloud passed under the moon and the world darkened as if a light had been turned off. The cloud moved on and the moon came out again, but only briefly. Soon it was darker than ever, and a streak of lightning cut across the sky to the west.

Derby Hat put more wood on the fire, and as the flames shot up, J.B. could again see the girl's face. She looked completely beaten.

"Where is it?" Derby Hat asked.

"I'll have to show you. You can't find it otherwise."

"You ain't showin' me nothin'. You'll tell me and you'll tell me right now."

"It's, uh, it's hidden in Juniper Canyon," she said. A sprinkling of cold raindrops fell. "It's hidden in a side canyon not far from the creek."

"Tell me how to find it."

The rain came down, causing the fire to sputter and finally go out. Derby Hat stood in front of the girl, trying to see her features. He shivered. Another streak of lightning lighted up the night for a second, followed by a loud clap of thunder. Derby Hat shivered again and looked around for something to cover himself with. "I never have a goddam slicker when I need one," he muttered.

J.B. turned his burning face up to the cold rain and got some relief. The girl shivered and dropped to the ground, sitting cross legged.

The lightning display continued and thunder boomed like a nearby cannon. The rain picked up. Derby Hat grabbed a piece of rope left behind by the other men and quickly tied the ankles of the two prisoners.

"You two can stay out here and drown," he said. "I'm goin' in." He patted the pistol on his hip. "One sound, one little move, and this old forty-four forty'll make mud holes in you." He walked rapidly to the cabin door and disappeared inside.

J.B. scooted over to the girl.

She whispered, "I guess you know he's going to kill us."

"I've been thinkin' about that."

"He has to kill us, you know."

"I've been thinkin' about that, too."

"Well?"

66

"Well what?" J.B. whispered. "Do you think I can just pop these ropes off and run?"

"You've got a terrific imagination, I can see that. Can't you think of something?"

"Listen, dammit." He almost apologized for his language, but decided not to. "Listen, I never saw your uncle or no money or no horse named Red Feather, or nothin'."

"I know that."

"You do?"

"Of course."

"Well, you're a pretty good actress yourself."

"A child could fool these gunsels."

"I've got an idea."

"Wonderful," she whispered, without enthusiasm.

Rain pounded down on them, and her blond hair was plastered to her head. Puddles formed around them. Between the flashes of lightning, the night was black. J.B. scooted on the seat of his pants until he was back to back with her, their hands touching. He whispered, "See if you can untie me."

She tried. Her fingers strained and pulled on the knot.

"The rope's wet. I can't seem to..." She strained some more. She said, "Damn it all anyway." A groan came out of her. "I'm not doing it, J.B. Maybe you can do better."

"I'd try, but my fingers are so numb I can't move 'em."

"Try anyway. Force yourself."

He tried. He concentrated on moving his index finger. "Move, dammit," he muttered. Finally, he got it to move, painfully. He concentrated on moving another finger. It moved. Then another. It felt as if hot needles were being stuck into them.

Soon he was able to move each finger. Then he went to work on her bonds. He silently cursed as he strained on a knot. It was ironic, he thought. The rain had driven their guard inside out of sight, but it had also made the grass rope difficult to untie. He got two fingers around a knot, pulled, and felt it loosen.

"You're doing it," she whispered, hope in her voice. He got one finger under a loop in the knot, strained, and pulled the end of the rope through the loop. The knot came unraveled easily after that.

67

"Now it's your turn again," he whispered.

She quickly untied her feet, got to her knees, and concentrated on untying his hands. "I wish that moon would come out so I could see, she said, whispering.

"Shhh," he cautioned. "Keep tryin'."

"I'm trying."

The rain came down.

He felt the knot loosen. She strained and pulled, her breath ragged in his ears. The knot loosened again. He was free. The pain he felt when he first moved his fingers was nothing compared to the pain that went through his hands as the blood rushed into them. He swung his hands several moments before he could manipulate them enough to untie his legs. He got unsteadily to his feet, and fell with a groan.

"Oh, your foot," she whispered, standing herself. "Can you stand at all?"

He got to his feet again and swayed unsteadily, putting nearly all his weight on his right foot.

"Do you think we can get away now?"

"I don't know." He looked around and picked up a length of firewood. He whispered to her, "You stand here and wait 'til I get beside the door, then make a racket. When he comes out, I'll knock 'im in the head."

"Can't we just slip away?"

"No. I don't want 'im shootin' at us."

J.B. hobbled slowly, painfully, with one boot on and the other off, to a spot beside the open door. "Now," he whispered.

She screamed. It started low, climbed to a high, eerie pitch, and subsided to a low growl, then climbed to an ear-splitting pitch again.

Nothing happened, and she screamed again. It sounded as if a herd of panthers were fighting and a couple of bears and an enraged bull or two had joined in. That did it.

Derby Hat bolted out the door, blinking his eyes and gripping the pistol. J.B. aimed for the back of his head and swung the firewood with both hands. Derby Hat staggered and fell on his face. J.B. hobbled painfully to him.

Before he could get there, the man rolled onto his back and started to get up. But the girl was on him from behind, grabbing the gun with both hands. He yanked on it, trying to wrestle it away from her. She hung on, desperately. J.B. hobbled toward them.

"Hurry," she yelled.

"I'm hurryin'."

He dropped astraddle of the man and got his hands on the gun. The man pitched and bucked and kept his hold. Miss Crandall was on her knees, astraddle his head.

"Sit on 'im," J.B. yelled.

"I'm sitting on him."

The pistol came free, and J.B. fell back onto the seat of his pants, turning the gun to a firing position as he fell. Miss Crandall slid away from the man, and he immediately started to get up. But when he found himself looking down the dangerous end of the gun, the fight was over.

"Just hold it right there," J.B. yelled. He realized his voice was at an abnormally high pitch and he tried to bring it down. "Don't move. Move and you're a dead man."

Miss Crandall stood beside J.B., holding her torn shirt together. For a while no one spoke. They were all panting for breath.

The rain slackened and stopped suddenly, as mountain rain squalls often do. The clouds moved on, and the moon came out again. J.B. looked at Miss Crandall. She looked at J.B. They were both muddy and disheveled from wrestling on the wet ground. J.B. grinned.

"If I ever hear of a screamin' contest, I'm gonna enter you in it."

She smiled slowly. "It wasn't all make-believe. What shall we do with him?" she asked, nodding at Derby Hat, whose hat had fallen off, revealing thick, iron-gray hair.

"What they done to us. Tie 'im up."

She picked up two lengths of rope from the ground and walked toward him. "Wait," J.B. said. "On your belly," he barked at the man. "Git on your belly and put your hands behind your back."

"Try'n make me," the man said, adding a string of obscenities.

J.B. did to the man what had been done to him. He placed the bore of the gun squarely between the man's eyes. His voice was hoarse with anger. "One little twitch of my finger and the top of your head'll be layin' in the mud. We've took a lot of abuse from you and your *compadres*, and I'd just as soon leave you dead. If I don't shoot you, Miss Crandall prob'ly will." He paused, "What'll it be, you woman-rapin' sonofabitch?"

Derby Hat did as ordered.

"Keep your face down too," the cowboy said. "Now," he said to the girl, "tie his hands and feet the way you'd tie a calf. And if he makes one move, I'll shoot holes in 'im."

She tied him. When she finished, J.B. hobbled over and inspected her work. He unbuckled the pistol belt, pulled it free, and tried to buckle it around his own waist, but he was too thin. The belt had cartridge loops built into it but contained only three cartridges. J.B. put them in his shirt pocket and threw the empty belt and holster toward the remains of the fire. The man cursed, spat dirt out of his mouth, and cursed some more.

J.B. sat on the ground and tried to pull on his left boot. He groaned and gave it up. She managed to button her shirt by putting buttons through mismatched buttonholes.

"All right," she said, "you can ride the one horse. I'll walk. Let's get moving." She was taking charge again.

J.B. picked up his empty boot and hobbled, painfully, toward the horse, carrying the six-gun in one hand and the boot in the other.

"Leave the boot," she said. "You've got enough to do to get yourself on that horse."

"These are good boots. I had 'em made to measure in Amarillo. And I'm gonna put my saddle on that horse. I ain't leavin' that behind either."

"I'll do it. But we have to get moving."

She untied the horse and led it over to where J.B.'s saddle lay on the ground. She shook and folded one of the Navaho blankets, put it on the horse's back and lifted the saddle up on top. J.B. hobbled over and cinched the saddle down tight.

"He's a gentle horse," he said. "Let's see if he'll carry double."

"If he bucks us off, we'll be afoot. And you with only one good leg."

"If I can get in that saddle, he ain't gonna buck me off."

He put his sore foot in the stirrup and tried to climb up. The

70

horse stood patiently, but J.B. couldn't put any weight on his burned foot.

"I'll help you," she said, lacing her fingers together to make a sling. "Put your knee in this."

With her help, he got into the saddle. "Now," he said, "you put your foot in the stirrup, grab my hand behind my back, and climb up." He handed her his right hand behind his back. She started to comply. "Wait," he said. "Hand me my boot." She did, and swung up onto the horse behind him. The horse stepped sideways and tried to jump, but J.B. held it in check.

"He'll get used to it," he said, and reined the horse away from the cabin, the dead fire, and the man lying tied on the ground. "Do you know this country?" he asked.

"I was up here once years ago when Uncle Len tried to buy it. It's awfully rough, but I think we can get down through Juniper Canyon over in that direction. That's the long way down, but we can't go back the way we came. We'd meet those men."

"That brings up another question. Where are we goin'?"

"To El Rey. We can't go to Raton now. We'd run into those men."

She was silent, thinking. "Looks like my only hope now is to get Sheriff White to try to solve the mystery of my uncle's disappearance."

"Goin' to El Rey's not such a good idea, not for me anyhow."

"Why? When I tell Sheriff White about John Buetel's hirelings, he'll forget about you. What they did to us was an outrage, and people around here won't stand for it."

"He won't forget me. That whole town's after my scalp."

"You said that before. And that man, the one with the slick moustache, he said something about your starting a stampede or something. What did you do, J.B.?"

He told her about it.

"You didn't!" she exclaimed, and J.B. detected a note of happiness in her voice. She asked for more, and he described it all. With every detail she chuckled. "J.B., you didn't. J.B., you're a hazard. Oh, I wish I could have seen it."

J.B. was happy about it because she was happy about it. "You should have seen ol' Derby Hat when he stepped out of the saloon and saw all them longhorns runnin' right at 'im. He let out a beller like a spooked squaw, and his shirt tail never hit his back 'till he was inside. And that woman that wanted to hang me, remember her? She was screamin', like the 'Paches had hold of her."

She punched him on the shoulder. "J.B., you're a caution."

"Well, anyhow, I'm a man with no place to go," said J.B., turning serious.

CHAPTER 7

They rode in silence across the wide valley. Soon the sky began to lighten, and the horizon to the east took on a dim glow. The horse, carrying a double load, was tiring. It stumbled twice.

"I think I had better get down and walk awhile," she said. J.B. looked down at his left foot, now blistering badly, and didn't argue. She walked and he rode and they covered several miles before the sun came up. Once, when they had to cross a swift mountain stream, she got back behind him on the horse and let the horse carry them both across. On the other side, she slid off the horse's rump and walked.

His burned foot hurt, but J.B. didn't mention it. At times he had to grit his teeth to hold back a groan. He tried to think of other things to get his mind off the pain. He looked down at the blond head of the girl walking alongside him and felt guilty about riding while she walked. J.B. smiled to himself when he remembered the way she had fought back there. And when the worst was about to happen, she hadn't begged, cried, or carried on at all. She was prepared to take whatever she had to take. He thought, If I had to git in a jackpot like this with a girl, I couldn't've picked a better one. There ain't any better ones.

She looked back, then glanced up at him. "I don't see anyone yet."

J.B. allowed they had a good head start, but with only one horse, the hoodlums could overtake them.

"They're probly startin' back up that canyon about now," he

said. "They now know I was tellin' stories about that money, and they'll be comin' for blood."

"They'll be desperate to catch up with us before we get to El Rey," she said, "And"—she swallowed—"they'll have to kill us to protect themselves."

"It's like you said back there, they intended to kill us anyway. All I did was buy us some time."

"I got you into a storm, didn't I, J.B.?" she said apologetically.

"Not as bad a storm as I was in back there in that jail. You don't owe me nothin'."

She walked along beside the horse and looked up at him with a half smile. "I'm glad you feel that way, J.B."

"Uh, Miss Crandall?"

"Shine."

"Uh, Shine, I still cain't figure out why you picked me to ride to Raton with you. You don't know me."

"I hate to travel alone. There are hoodlums in New Mexico Territory, as we just found out, and there was no one else. Oh, Joel probably would have traveled with me if I had asked him to, but he has a future on the CC if he doesn't put off the new owners, and he is soon to be married. I couldn't ask him to leave. He's been a loyal employee, but I didn't want to jeopardize his future. I'm sure his fiancée wouldn't approve of his riding off with another woman either."

J.B. chuckled. "But I had nothin' to lose, is that it?"

She looked up at him on the horse and smiled again. "Well, it's the truth, isn't it?"

They had crossed the valley and were in the thick timber, mostly lodgepole pines and ponderosas, with a few aspens. The grass was tall, and wild flowers of all colors were everywhere. The girl pointed to a line of willows ahead and said that had to be where Juniper Creek began picking up volume. The creek tumbled down a long, deep canyon and splashed right past the CC Ranch buildings, she said. "It's that creek that makes the CC so valuable."

They followed a cattle trail to the creek, pushed their way through several acres of dense willows, and then turned downstream. "I rode down this canyon a few years ago with my uncle and two cowboys," the girl said. "It's rough terrain, but a horse can make it."

"Let's git out of these willers, and see if we can find a trail," the cowboy suggested.

"Yes, I believe the best trail is on the other side."

He offered her his right hand behind his back again, and she climbed up behind him. The horse groaned at the added weight, but carried them safely across the roiling creek.

"I sure wish we could let this horse rest and graze awhile," said J.B., "but we have to keep goin'."

They kept going, the girl walking and the injured cowboy riding. The canyon was wide and shallow at the upper end, but soon, after they had traveled downhill a half mile, the horse had to clamber over rocks and cross the creek in several places. Miss Crandall had to climb down hand over hand at times.

The creek picked up volume as small streams fed into it, and soon it became swift enough to knock a man off his feet if he dared step in. Miss Crandall had to climb up onto the horse to get across.

Now they were deep inside a canyon with walls that rose almost straight up for two hundred feet. A bald eagle soared overhead and let out a screech as if it didn't approve of the people below. The trail gave out completely in places. Miss Crandall blamed the recent rains for washing out the trail and turning the creek into a torrent, making travel much more hazardous than it had been a few years earlier.

They hadn't traveled two miles down the canyon when the horse slipped on a wet rock and went down on its haunches. It stayed right side up, however, and quickly scrambled to its feet. J.B. kept his seat, but he was worried that the horse was getting weak from exhaustion and hunger.

"We're gonna have to stop someplace, he said. "Their horses are tired, too, tireder than this one."

She was breathing heavily from the exertion of climbing and sliding, and she talked between breaths. "We'll...have to stop...before dark... We can't find...our way out...of here in the dark."

"How far to the bottom?"

"It's a good twenty miles... We'll never make it...before dark."

"Well, ol' horse," J.B. said, "it won't be long 'till we'll have to stop and let you rest."

It wasn't much later than midafternoon, it seemed, when the sun went out of sight over the western rim, and it was about then that the horse fell again.

J.B. rolled clear and wasn't hurt. He staggered up, stood on his one good foot, and pulled on the horse's head to get it up. The animal rose, slowly, and stood swaybacked. "I sure hate to do this to a horse," the cowboy said.

"It's a matter of life and death," Miss Crandall commented. "Our lives and our deaths."

"I promise you, ol' horse, if we get out of this alive, I'll see you have a long rest and plenty of feed, even if I have to steal you to do it."

With her help, he got back on the horse, and they traveled on.

But the next time the horse fell, it almost didn't stand up again. It was at a place where the canyon wall sloped gently, and where a fingerlike low ridge sloped down to the water's edge. They stopped and tried to find a way over the ridge. "I can climb over," she said, "but I'm not so sure a horse can."

The cowboy sat in the saddle and looked it over. He looked into the water, which was deep at that point, and he looked up at the canyon rim: not too high, but too steep to climb. Could the horse make it? A good strong horse could make it easy enough if the dirt was solid, he thought. But one that was weak from hunger and fatigue? J.B. considered getting down and turning the horse loose and crawling over the ridge. Hell, if the horse failed to get across, he would be on foot anyway.

"What do you think, J.B.?"

"If I try, I might be put afoot," he answered slowly, thoughtfully. "If I don't try, I sure will be afoot. Well, I always said I could ride a horse anyplace I could walk, and I never got down and led a horse in my life, not even when I had two good feet." He urged the horse forward.

The animal hesitated a moment, then did as the human on its back told it to. It got its front feet up onto the side of the ridge, and then got its hind feet up. It paused as if to say it knew better than to go forward, but it went forward.

The distance over the foot of the ridge was only about thirty feet, and for a while it looked as if the horse would make it. But then a large rock moved under a front hoof, and immediately the remainder of the ridge under the horse's feet caved off into the creek.

J.B. was afraid that would happen, and he was ready. He pitched himself to the left of the horse and fell clear. He grabbed the trunk of a small juniper and held on.

The horse landed on its back in the water, but managed to get up and scramble onto dry land before it collapsed. The six-gun J.B. had been carrying inside his belt fell out and slid downhill. It stopped short of the water. The boot he had been carrying went into the water and floated downstream before it disappeared.

Miss Crandall was behind J.B. She kept quiet until it was all over and the dirt and rocks stopped sliding. Then she asked calmly, "Can you make it over the hump, J.B.?"

"I can make it," he said through clenched teeth. "You'll have to crawl."

"I can crawl." He crawled on his hands and knees to where the horse lay on its side, and looked back at the girl. "Can you get the gun? We might need it."

"I can get it."

She too was crawling, and she reached down for the gun, grabbed it by the handle, and crawled on her knees and one hand. When she reached J.B., she sat on the ground beside him. Both stared at the prone horse. The animal lay on its side, and its right leg was bent at a sharp angle below the knee. It was groaning. The cowboy put his face in his hands, and when he spoke his voice was muffled. "I never killed a horse before." She touched his arm.

Slowly, woodenly, lips clamped shut, he reached for the gun. He cocked the hammer back, saw the cylinder turn to place a bullet under the hammer. Still moving as if in a trance, he stood up and hobbled over to the horse's head. "I'd rather not send a signal to old Derby Hat, but I cain't let that horse suffer."

"Wait a minute, will you?" the girl asked quietly. She got up and walked down the narrow trail and stopped. She kept her back to J.B. and the horse.

J.B. imagined a large X running between the horse's ears and eyes. He put the end of the barrel a few inches from where the imaginary X crossed, and pulled the trigger.

The shot boomed and echoed up and down the canyon walls. The horse felt no pain. The cowboy did.

He stood with head bowed, then half walked and half hopped to where the girl was waiting. His voice was strained. "I hoped I would never, ever have to do that."

She spoke softly. "It had to be done. I'm sorry I got you into this, J.B. I'm terribly sorry."

"You're not to blame for anything, Miss Crandall. Not one thing. None of this is your fault."

He looked for a piece of driftwood or a piñon limb that would make a crutch. He found nothing better than a short piece of driftwood that he could use for a walking stick. With Miss Crandall in the lead, he hobbled painfully down the narrow, and at times nonexistent, trail. Once he stopped and looked back. "I hate to leave my saddle there."

"We'll come back for it. I promise."

Just before dark they came to a short pocket in the canyon wall and decided to rest. Neither had eaten since noon the day before, and hunger was constantly gnawing at their insides. They built a fire, which warmed them up. They hoped the moon would put out enough light that they could continue their journey. Meanwhile, they sat by the fire.

She tried to be cheerful. "As my dad used to say when he was hungry, 'My stomach thinks my throat's been cut.'"

He grinned weakly. "My big guts're eatin' up my little ones."

"At least we're alive," she said. "This time yesterday, I thought we had only a few hours to live. If that long."

She stood up suddenly and walked toward a clump of willow bushes at the back end of the pocket.

"What's up?" he asked.

She answered with that half smile, "When a lady heads for the bushes, don't ask questions."

"Oh, excuse me."

She rinsed her hands in the creek when she came back and sat beside him. They were silent a moment, then she said, "Tell me about yourself, J.B. Where were you raised?"

"I wasn't raised, I was fetched up."

She chuckled. "I gather your family isn't, uh, exactly affluent."

"They didn't have much money, either," he said. He paused. "They were farmers. My two brothers still are. But they never had a piece of land that would graze a goat, and ever' cotton boll they got they earned two or three times."

"I knew you were from Texas the first time I saw you."

"When you're fetched up in South Texas you don't know how to talk like a Yankee."

She threw her head back and laughed. "Miss Crandall?"

"Shine."

"Excuse me. Shine. One of those yahoos, the one with the Derby Hat, said somethin' last night that's got me thinkin'."

"What's that?"

"He said somethin' about ol' Buetel wantin' me hanged. Didn't you say ol' Derby Hat worked for Buetel?"

"Yes. He and the other man. The only one of the three I didn't recognize is the one with the long black coat. Buetel has a ranch just downstream from ours—it's the Box O—and lately he has hired some rough-looking characters."

"The CC headquarters is right at the bottom of this canyon, ain't it?"

"Yes. That gives us control of the water that comes down Juniper Creek. We use that water to good advantage. We irrigate about two hundred acres of good meadowland and raise hay for the winter. If we had kept the ranch, we would eventually have irrigated more land."

"A meadowland is what we call a vega, ain't it?"

"Yes. Most New Mexicans call it a vega too."

"How did your dad and uncle come by the CC?"

"They started with two homesteads. Then they hired men to homestead more acres adjacent to theirs, and bought them out. That was cheaper than buying it from the government, but they bought governmental land too until they had nearly four sections. That, with the open range, gave them enough grass to raise about five hundred calves a year.

"They worked hard, seldom hired any help, and plowed all profits back into land and more cows to raise more calves. Then somehow my dad suspected, long before anyone else did, that the railroad was coming over Raton Pass and would go through our part of the country. He bought like crazy. He had to borrow to do it. And sure enough, just last year the railroad company completed laying track. Until then, we had to go to Raton for supplies. But since the railroad came through, the new town of El Rey has sprung up, mostly financed by the bank, and the value of land around here has soared. And now that the open range is being claimed and fenced, land values are going even higher."

She grew pensive suddenly. "The sad part is, just before my dad could realize the wisdom of buying land in preparation for the railroad, he and my mother were killed. They were coming back from Raton with a wagonload of supplies when a band of marauding Apaches attacked and killed them. The soldiers chased the Indians back to their reservation, but didn't punish them."

A bitter note crept into her voice. "The federal government thinks it has mistreated the Indians, so it's going to make everyone else pay for it."

"I'm sorry about your folks."

"It was so unfair. They worked so hard, and they had one of the finest small ranches in the New Mexico Territory."

"How did the bank happen to have a mortgage on it?"

"Dad took out the first mortgage with the bank in Santa Fe, but the papers were transferred last year to the new Piñon Valley National Bank in El Rey. Then Uncle Len wanted more land and he took out another mortgage. Oh, I can't say it was his fault. It was a wise investment. It paid off. It was just, well, Uncle Len's eccentricities that cost us the ranch. His distrust of banks. He hated bankers but he liked being able to borrow money. He kept skipping mortgage payments. He said he would soon pay off the whole note, and he had the money to do it. When we sent nine carloads of beeves to Denver a week ago, Uncle Len made them pay him in cash.

"The last time I saw Uncle Len he was carrying two saddlebags of paper money and a small pouch of gold in his slicker. He said he was going to El Rey to pay off the mortgage. I remember his exact words: 'I'm gonna git that dang banker off my neck.' That's what he said."

"And," J.B. concluded, "because he disappeared with the money, you couldn't pay off the mortgage, and the bank foreclosed."

"Yes, but"—she threw her head back and shook the blond hair out of her eyes—"no one need worry about me. I can take care of myself."

A steady pain throbbed through J.B.'s left foot and the left side of his face, and he hobbled to the creek and put his foot in the cold water. He splashed water on his face and went back to their camp. She got up, broke a branch of a stunted piñon, picked up a piece of driftwood, and fed the fire.

"You're in pain, aren't you?"

"I'll live."

She sat and scratched the ground with the end of a twig. Suddenly she threw the twig in the fire and said through clenched teeth, "No one has ever treated a member of my family or one of my friends the way they treated us, and by God, no one is going to do it and live to tell about it."

He was surprised at her blasphemy and said so.

"I can swear in two languages when I want to, and once in a while I want to." She picked up another stick and jabbed at the ground with it. "Right now I'm more determined than ever to find out what happened to Uncle Len. If he left the country with all our money, I'm going to track him down and get my share. My folks worked just as hard for the ranch as he did, and half that money is mine. And if he didn't run out, then, by God, I want to know what happened to him and who did it. And when I find out, some *hijo de puta* is going to suffer."

She stood up. "Do you feel like moving on? I'm too mad to rest, and the moon's up now."

She strode out ahead of him, then stopped and waited for him to catch up. "I'm sorry," she said, "but anger gets my adrenaline flowing and I can't sit still."

"Gits your what flowin'?"

"My adrenaline. There's no other word for it. You know what it means."

"I can guess. Listen, Miss Crandall—"

"Shine. Shine, do you understand?"

"Listen, Shine, I'd advise you to go on ahead of me, but there's no tellin' who you might run into before we get down on the flats. Those hooligans are after us, no doubt about that, and I was thinkin' if I was them, I'd maybe send two men down this trail after us and another around the rim to come up at us from below."

"You could be right." she said. "If their horses don't give out, they could head us off."

"We've got two things goin' for us," the cowboy added. He held up the gun. "This, and bein' afoot. Afoot, we can hide and be hard to find. I think maybe sometime before daylight we ought to find a place to climb out of this canyon and git up on the rim where we can maybe see them before they see us. If they catch up with us down here, we could be trapped, bottled up. I could maybe git one of 'em with this pistol, but they've got at least one rifle and that sure gives 'em an advantage."

She studied his face, thinking about what he had said.

"I think we'd have a better chance up there."

"You're right," she said with finality. "That's what we'll do."

CHAPTER 8

They hadn't traveled another hour—her walking and climbing briskly and him hobbling, skipping, and grimacing—when the sky clouded over again and another cold rain fell. They huddled under a rock overhang, but it provided little protection, and within minutes they were soaked. Fatigue eventually overcame their discomfort, and they dozed fitfully. That is, J.B. dozed fitfully. She dozed peacefully. She had sat hugging her knees and then slumped over against the cowboy.

J.B. studied her face in the meager light. With her face relaxed and with her long feminine eyelashes, he again wondered how he had ever mistaken her for a boy. He forgot his pain as his protective instincts took over. It was an almost paternal instinct. He wished he could dry her off and cover her with something warm, and drive away all her problems.

It was hard to believe, he thought, that this was the girl who fought like a wildcat when Derby Hat had hit him, who jumped up immediately when she was knocked down and continued her assault, who told, not asked, the High Sheriff of the County what to do. And this was the girl who, if the missing money could be found, would be the boss of the CC Ranch.

He had known feisty women before, but Miss Crandall was the first he had known who could talk like a lady and fight like crazy all in the same day. And wasn't that a rotten break she got? Had a half interest in what looks to be a hell of a good little cow outfit and lost it all at once. Brought up a ranch owner's daughter and now having to look for a job. Lost her folks and now her home. Most men, if they had lost what she lost, would booze themselves to death or spend the rest of their lives bellyachin' about their bad luck.

She could smile about it and laugh at things. Had to force herself to smile, he knew, but at least she had enough guts to force herself. And she was no hard-hearted witch. She hated what happened to that horse as much as he did, and he had been accused of liking horses better than people. And that wasn't too far from the truth.

Not only that, she was about the prettiest girl he had ever seen. He would like to see her in a party dress. He'd bet she could have men standin' on their heads to show off to her. He was thinking thoughts like that when she stirred.

When she found herself leaning against him, her cheek on his shoulder, she straightened up suddenly. "I slept, didn't I?" she said, as if she had done something wrong.

Grinning crookedly, he answered, "Yeah, a little. Sleep some more if you want to."

"Oh, no," she said, standing up. "We might as well be making tracks. We're wet anyway."

As before, the rain was a short one, and soon the clouds moved eastward and the full moon resumed its duties. The farther down the canyon they got, the better the trail became, and that worried J.B. If their antagonists were coming up the trail after them, they would all meet within the next few hours. He kept looking up at the canyon wall and trying to decide whether his thinking earlier that night had been logical. Hell, he was no soldier, and he couldn't be sure about what was the best thing to do.

Would it be better to shoot it out with them here on the canyon bottom where they could hide behind boulders, or to get up on the rim? Here, as long as one of them could shoot, nobody was going to get across that creek and get around behind them. But in all probability, one or two of Beutel's men were already coming down. Another could climb up on the rim and shoot from above.

They had better fortifications below, but they couldn't escape either. J.B. reached a decision, and he touched the girl on the arm to get her attention.

"Soon's we come to a place where we can climb, let's git out of this gulch."

"Yes," she said looking up at the canyon walls, "if it comes to a gunfight, we'll be fish in a barrel."

"You're a soldier too?" He grinned crookedly.

Her return smile flashed on and off. "I've got a strong sense of self-preservation. Are you a good shot?"

"Have to be. I shot rabbits on the run when I was a kid. Had to, to eat."

"I have to admit I've never fired a weapon much, but I can shoot if I have to."

It was breaking daylight when they got to where the canyon walls sloped enough for them to climb. She went first, grabbing hold of the stunted junipers, bunch grass, and anything else she could get her hands on. He followed, carrying the six-gun. He had to discard his makeshift walking stick. Once she slipped and slid down against him, and he gave her a shove back up. It wasn't until it was too late that he realized he had put his hands on her rump. He would have been embarrassed if she had said anything. But if she noticed, she didn't let on.

They had to pause twice to get their breath. But clambering and scrambling, pulling and pushing, grunting and heaving, they finally got to the top.

Standing with most of his weight on one foot, J.B. looked over the terrain. They were on top of a mesa, the kind of flat-topped hill that was common in northern New Mexico Territory, only this one covered a dozen square miles. J.B. hoped that the east side was not as steep as the side they had climbed up. With a practiced eye, he noticed that the tall bunch grass had been grazed off in places, and that, plus year-old cattle droppings, was an indication that the east side was easy to climb. Vegetation other than the tall grass was scarce. A few outcroppings of granite was scattered over the terrain.

They sat with their backs to an outcropping until their breathing returned to normal. They could see most of the canyon floor from there, and they saw no sign of life. It would be nice, J.B. thought, if Derby Hat and company went on up the canyon looking for them. That way, they could sneak in behind them and go on down to wherever they were going. But he doubted that would happen. If those men had any rangeland savvy at all, they would see where the two had climbed out of the canyon. It was impossible to cover their tracks.

J.B. had known all along that they would more than likely have to shoot their way past those men, and he was trying to think of a way to communicate that to the girl. She solved the problem herself.

"How many cartridges are in that gum" she asked.

J.B. flipped open the loading gate and counted the bullets. "Four," he said. "He must of kept an empty under the hammer. And I've got three in my pocket. These forty-four forties hit hard, but I'd sure like to trade this six-gun for a rifle."

"Unless they get help from the ranch, there will be only three men after us," she said, "but you can't waste too many shots."

"I know that," he said.

"I know you know that." She was looking off into space.

He gave her a hard look but she didn't see it. She just couldn't help being the boss, he thought.

After a short rest, they went on, keeping near the edge of the rim so they could see down into the canyon. J.B. found another stick he could use to help him hobble along. His left foot was blistered badly, but he believed, when he thought about it, that the pain had subsided a little.

The sun was up, and it was going to be a hot day. The cowboy missed his hat. He couldn't remember ever being outdoors before without a hat. He was worried about whether they could get past the men and where they would go if they got past them. He was worried about his custom-made saddle back on the canyon trail under a dead horse. He had always said he would ride any kind of a horse but he was particular about his saddle. He was even worried about his left boot, which was probably at the bottom of the creek, filled with sand and gravel.

A loud splashing in the creek below stopped them in their tracks and brought about a quick exchange of glances. "It's them," he said. Bent low, they walked to the edge of the rim and looked down.

The trail crossed the creek below them. Two men were riding across. It was Derby Hat and the gambler. They were riding upstream, which meant they had come from the lower end of the canyon. It also meant the third man was coming down the canyon and was somewhere behind J.B. and the girl.

But the fact that Derby Hat and the gambler were alone was good news too. At least J.B. could hope it was. Since they came from the direction of the CC Ranch, it could mean they had not gone to the ranch for help.

The two men stopped their horses on the other side of the creek and studied the trail. It was obvious to them that their quarry had not passed there. Derby Hat pushed his hat back on his head and studied the canyon walls. J.B. and the girl were lying on their stomachs peering down at them. They jerked their heads back out of sight.

J.B. knew what he ought to do. He ought to shoot them right there. They were out in the open where he couldn't miss. If he shot them right there, the battle would be nearly over.

He looked down again. The men were riding on, Derby Hat in the lead. He cocked the hammer back and sighted along the pistol barrel. Let's see, which one first. Ol' Derby Hat, the one who had started to molest the girl. He fitted the front sight into the notch of the rear sight right in the middle of Derby Hat's back. The girl spoke.

"You're not going to...? Yes, that's the thing to do. Do it."

Her voice broke his aim, and he looked up at her. "It's the smart thing to do," he said defensively.

"Do it. They would do it to us."

"I'm goin' to." He drew a bead on the man's back again. His finger tightened on the trigger. It was about fifty feet, and he couldn't miss.

J.B. had never pointed a gun at a man before. He knew that if the time ever came when he had to shoot or be shot, he would shoot. And he knew that those men intended to kill him and the girl. Not only that, if ol' Derby Hat had his way, he would have his pleasure with the girl before he killed her. They didn't deserve to live. They were worse than rattlesnakes and Apaches and boll weevils and anything else.

"Shoot," she said.

He turned on his side and pushed the pistol toward her. "You shoot."

"Not me. I can't."

"Well, I cain't either. I cain't shoot a man that ain't even lookin' at me."

"It's the smart thing to do."

"I know it's the smart thing to do. But whoever said ol' J.B. Watts was smart?"

For a moment, they glared at each other. When he looked back over the edge, he saw the two men ride out of sight around the bend in the creek.

He stood up and staggered on his one good foot for a second until he got his balance.

She stood up too.

"I know I'm dumb and stupid and ain't got the brains of a sledgehammer, but I just cain't shoot a man in the back."

"I don't blame you."

"You don't?"

"No."

"You sure?"

"I don't blame you, J.B. I couldn't have done it either."

He let the hammer down gently on the gun and picked up his walking stick.

"We have to get going," she said.

"That's what I was about to say." His voice was gruff.

She took the lead at first, then stopped and waited for him to catch up. When he did, she took his arm and tried to help him walk. "No," he said, "I can make it."

"Are you mad at me, J.B.?"

"No. No, I guess I'm just mad at myself. I could have knocked off two-thirds of our troubles back there."

She faced him and smiled a tight smile. "Forget it, J.B."

He knew she was forcing herself to smile again, and he felt another spark of admiration for her. He managed to grin, "Shine, you're a caution."

They followed the edge of the mesa, close to the canyon rim, hoping the east side wasn't too far away. It was near midday when they heard a noise from the bottom. J.B. crawled on his hands and knees to the edge and peered over. He found himself facing Derby Hat, not more than fifty yards away.

"There they are," the man yelled. J.B. pulled his head back. He looked around.

"We've got to find a place to take a stand. They'll be comin' up here after us now."

She looked around too and pointed downhill. "There's a pile of boulders. It's ideal."

It was, in fact. It was a small but high outcropping of granite near the edge of the canyon rim and a good six hundred yards from any other cover. But it was a quarter of a mile away.

Without a word J.B. started hobbling toward it, grimacing with pain. She took his arm. "Let me help, will you?"

"You take the gun," he said, "and go on in case they get up here before I get over there."

"No. It will take them a while to find a way out of that canyon. We'll make it."

"Take the gun and go on, will you?"

"No."

He soon found that she was more help than the walking stick. He dropped it, put his left arm around her shoulders, and limped on. He expected to see two men on horseback galloping toward them any minute. If they were caught out in the open, it would be two guns, including at least one rifle, against one pistol. They needed the advantage of those rocks.

Every time his left foot touched the ground, pain ran through it, but he decided the pain was better than death, and he went on. They almost made it.

"Here they come," she said.

They were coming, riding hard, right at them. Derby Hat had a rifle in his hand. The gambler had a six-gun. It was obvious they had guessed where J.B. and the girl were headed and they were trying to cut them off.

"Run for those rocks, Shine," J.B. said. "Don't wait for me."

"No."

"All right then, hit the ground. On your belly." She did as he ordered.

J.B. dropped to one knee and cocked the pistol. Derby Hat with his rifle would be the most dangerous and would be his first target, he decided. He supported his gun arm by resting his elbow on his knee and holding his right wrist with his left hand. He fired.

Derby Hat brought his horse to a stop, but he was still in the saddle, and J.B. knew he had missed. He knew the gun fired ammunition that wouldn't carry that far. But the shot had made the horsemen stop. They were no longer charging toward them.

"Let's try again," J.B. said.

The girl jumped up, grabbed J.B. by the arm, and together they went for the boulders. A bullet hit a small rock in front of them and ricocheted off over the canyon. A split second later the shot was heard. Derby Hat was firing.

"Damn," said J.B. "We're a good target for that long gun."

"That gives us no choice but to run for it," she said, excitement in her voice. "We have to keep running."

Another shot. The bullet hit the ground and kicked up a puff of dust. Derby Hat's gun had the range, but the shooter had not yet figured out the elevation, J.B. knew. But he knew the shooter would soon do that.

The next shot was close enough that the girl and the crippled cowboy heard it go past.

Half running and dragging his left foot, J.B. hurried on. The rocks were not far ahead. Derby Hat spurred his horse toward them again. So did the gambler, and the gambler was firing his six-gun as he charged.

J.B. had to stop them again or at least slow them down. He dropped to one knee again, held the pistol in both hands straight out in front of him, and took aim. He aimed high, hoping the bullet would drop close enough to the target to make the man cautious. He squeezed the trigger.

The Derby Hat went spinning and the man fell onto the neck of his horse.

"You got him, J.B." The girl was excited, still standing.

He looked over at her. "Git down, Shine." When he looked back he saw with dismay that Derby Hat, though hatless, was still on his horse and was bringing the horse to a stop. He had hit the hat without hitting the man.

"Damn," he said again.

The gambler was firing his pistol, but the bullets were falling short. Derby Hat was off his horse now and obviously not hurt. He too dropped onto one knee.

"Down," J.B. yelled. He and the girl both fell onto their stomachs at the same instant the man fired. The bullet went over them.

"Now run," J.B. said.

They were both on their feet instantly, and she pulled J.B. by the arm, trying to help him. The hoodlum fired again, but this time he didn't take careful aim and the bullet went harmlessly over the canyon.

The gambler was still riding recklessly toward them, intending to get within easy pistol range before they got to the rocks. One of his bullets hit the ground with a thud ahead of them, and another hit a small rock so close that it sprayed gravel onto J.B.'s right leg.

"Run," he yelled at the girl. "Go on."

"No." She continued half carrying him.

The gambler had to stop to reload, but Derby Hat was taking aim again.

"Dive," J.B. yelled. They both hit the ground face down at the instant Derby Hat fired, then jumped up immediately.

"We're...going to...make it," the girl said.

J.B. clenched his teeth and tried to ignore the pain as he hurried. A bullet screamed off the pile of rocks just as they got there. They fell behind the rocks and lay on the ground, breathing hard.

They were safe for only a moment, J.B. knew. They, rather he, had to shoot back. He had to look over the top of the outcropping and shoot to keep the men from getting closer. He stood up. If he'd waited two more seconds, it would have been too late.

The gambler had reloaded his six-gun and was riding at them again, shooting. J.B. remembered that the gambler was carrying two six-guns when he last saw him and he wondered why he had only one now. But he didn't wonder about it very long. A bullet whined over J.B.'s head, and another smacked against the rocks near his head. J.B. fought down the instinct to duck. He took aim. No elevation was needed this time.

The shot boomed, the gun barrel kicked up. A split second later the gambler threw up his hands, dropped his pistol, and rolled backward off the horse. He hit the ground on his back, feet in the air. The horse veered to its right and kept running. The man lay still.

"Got him." It was the girl, standing beside J.B.

"For gawd's sake," he said to her, "git down."

She ignored him. "It's an even fight now," she said.

"Yeah, 'til that other man catches up."

"At least the odds are better."

"Yeah, but that feller's still got that long gun and this pistol's no match for it."

It occurred to J.B. that he had just killed a man. For the first time in his life, he had shot and killed a human being. Then he saw what Derby Hat was doing, and he forgot about it.

The man was leading his horse but keeping it between him and the rocks. Then the horse was freed and it walked away, dragging its bridle reins. Derby Hat was not in sight.

"Damn," said J.B. "There cain't be more'n one draw within six hundred yards out there and he's found that one." The draw, or gulley, was a shallow, narrow one, but deep enough that a man could lie out of sight in it. It was too far away for an accurate pistol shot, but J.B. guessed that by allowing for elevation he could drop a bullet close enough to keep the man from being too bold.

Derby Hat's rifle barrel could be seen sticking up out of the gulley, but the man couldn't be seen. It was a standoff.

J.B. looked around. They were in a good spot. Their fortress was near enough to the edge of the canyon rim that no one could get behind them. They would be hard to hit behind the rocks.

The girl said aloud what J.B. had been thinking. "We're fairly safe here, but we're stuck here. This isn't getting us out of our predicament."

"I've been thinkin' about that," he said. "It's just a matter of time 'til that other man gits here. He'll come along and see where we climbed up, then he'll see where them two turned back and climbed up theirselves, and he'll foller their tracks."

"I know. It will take him a while to find a way around the spot where that dead horse is, but he'll get here eventually."

Conversation ceased for a time. J.B. kept his eyes glued to the draw where Derby Hat was hidden. He had four shots left, and he would soon be facing two men. He wished he had another gun. With another gun, maybe the girl could keep Derby Hat's head down while he got to where he could pick him off. Or...That gave him an idea.

The gambler's horse was hungrily cropping the bunch grass not far from where J.B. and the girl stood behind their fortress. If the girl could take the gun and keep Derby Hat's head down, maybe he could catch that horse and...and what?

He couldn't go for help. He'd be shot on sight if he rode into El Rey. Besides, he couldn't leave the girl here alone. She spoke.

"I've got an idea J.B."

"What?"

"I can catch that horse and go for help. You can keep that man from shooting at me."

J.B. was astonished. For a moment he just gawked at her.

"He doesn't dare raise up out there. If he did, you couldn't miss. He knows that. It would be easy."

"No, you cain't do that. I cain't let you."

"Let me?" Her eyebrows went up. "I'm a spoiled landowner's daughter. Do you know how long it's been since anyone 'let me' do anything?"

"You cain't do it."

"It's our only chance, J.B. I can get on that horse and ride for El Rey. I'll get some help and come back."

"Listen, Miss Crandall. Shine. That other feller'll be comin' along anytime now, and if you run into him he'll chop you up in little pieces."

"You listen, cowboy. I know that horse over there. That's a CC horse. He's gentle and he's fast. I've ridden him many times, and there isn't a better horse in the world at a time like this. I can ride him bareback, and with so little weight he'll leave that other man's horse choking on the dust."

"You cain't ride bareback that far." J.B. was trying desperately to talk her out of it.

"I rode bareback all the time when I was a child."

He tried to find other ways to discourage her, but he could only sputter.

"Keep your eye on that man, J.B. I'll be back. I promise, I'll be back." She walked away toward the grazing horse.

The cowboy stared at her, then suddenly remembered what he had to do. He turned his attention back to Derby Hat just in time. The man was pointing his rifle at the girl.

J.B. had no time to take aim. He snapped a shot and saw it kick up dirt close to Derby Hat's face. The man wasn't hit, but the shot spoiled his aim. He immediately ducked back into his gulley.

Afraid to blink, J.B. kept all his attention on the draw where he knew Derby Hat was hiding. He wanted to see how the girl was, but he knew he would be jeopardizing her life if he as much as glanced her way. The pistol was in J.B.'s hands and his hands were resting on top of a boulder. He kept the front sight between the V in the rear sight a little over Derby Hat's hiding place. Uh oh, movement. Derby Hat raised his head, then raised his rifle.

J.B. let him get the gun to his shoulder, then fired.

The man suddenly dropped the rifle as if it had burned his hands. He swore so loudly that J.B. could hear every word. He picked up the gun and tried to jack the lever down, but the lever was stuck. J.B. felt like letting out a whoop. He had missed the man but he had hit the gun. Derby Hat's rifle was out of action.

The girl had seen what happened. She yelled, "Good shooting, J.B."

But the danger wasn't over. Derby Hat was afraid to show his head, but his hand with a pistol in it appeared out of the draw. J.B. guessed he had borrowed one of the gambler's pearl-handled six-guns. He yelled back at the girl, "Be careful, he's got another gun."

Not only did he have another gun, J.B. knew the pistol, though not as accurate, was faster than the rifle had been. He had to keep the man down. Couldn't let him even flicker an eyelash. He drew a bead on the spot where Derby Hat would have to show if he dared.

Miss Crandall rode past at a gallop. She was riding bareback. She flashed a smile and waved, but J.B. didn't see her. He was concentrating on his own duty.

Not until he heard the hoofbeats recede did he dare look after her. The horse was running easily. He watched them until they disappeared in the distance.

CHAPTER 9

It was suddenly very quiet on the canyon rim where J.B. Watts waited behind a rock fortress. He could relax for a while. Ol' Derby Hat wouldn't dare rush him. He was safe until the third man arrived, and he hoped that wouldn't be for a long time. It occurred to J.B. that his burned foot was no longer hurting. But then how could it, with so much happening. It also occurred to him that he was terribly hungry.

How long could a man go without eating? And drinking? He could use some water too. Hell, a long time. The greatest danger he faced came from his antagonists, not from starvation. He was made to realize that a man could go longer without eating than without sleeping. Gawd, he was sleepy. He longed to sit on the ground behind his rocks and catch a few winks. Ol' Derby Hat wasn't gonna do a thing until he got some help. Hell, why not?

Why not? Because when ol' Derby Hat's *compadre* came, J.B. didn't want to be caught napping, that's why not. He had to stay awake.

He waited, fighting to keep his eyes open. How long had it been? Three nights. He hadn't slept for three nights. His mind wandered, imagining the girl riding as hard as the horse could run to get away from the man with "Ed" painted on his batwing chaps. He worried. Maybe that's why he hasn't showed up here. He's after her. Ride, Miss Crandall. If anything happened to that girl, J.B. would spend the rest of his life, if necessary, catching up with whoever hurt her. He'd shoot them down like calf-killing coyotes. Hell, he had more respect for coyotes. They had to kill to live. How in hell did the world get so bollixed up anyway? Kill to live. What kind of scheme is that? J.B. realized his mind was wandering too far, getting close to crazy thoughts. The need for sleep must be driving him out of his mind.

He slapped his face a stinging blow, hoping the pain would force his mind to alertness. If he didn't get some sleep soon, he'd be a dead man.

Think about something else. Chances are that girl is all right. What else? That poker game. The one that left him with nothing but a horse and saddle. Let's see. Yep, one of the gamblers looked almost exactly like that dead man over there. That long black coat, those pearl-handled six-shooters. Seems to be a kind of uniform for gamblers. He's the one who had four aces, the last poker hand J.B. ever saw. Four aces? What are the chances of anybody drawing four aces? He was cheating. He dealt J.B. kings full and then dealt himself four aces. Hell, those yahoos can deal from the bottom of the deck or the middle or anywhere else. And J.B. had been dumb. Just another dumb cowpuncher.

When the gambler raised him, J.B. was elated. They couldn't beat kings full. And when that slick sonofabitch grinned that egg-sucking grin and said J.B. was bluffing and raised him again, J.B. knew he was going to win a hell of a jackpot. It was his chance to get back what he'd lost. He didn't even count his remaining chips, he just shoved them into the middle of the table and said, "See you and add this."

The gambler was a cool one. He put on quite an act, pretending to think it over and shaking his head, and allowing as how he still thought the cowboy was bluffing. He called.

Hell, now that J.B. was thinking about it, the gambler wasn't gambling at all. He knew what J.B. had and he knew what he had.

Nobody but a dumb, stupid, manure-for-brains cowpuncher would play cards with a professional gambler. But that was a lesson many a man had to learn the hard way. Well, J.B. had learned his lesson, and he would know better in the future.

If he had a future.

Stay awake. He looked up at the sky, saw the white clouds

drifting slowly eastward, wondered if they would get together, turn dark, and spill rain on him again. The sky was the bluest he had ever seen. And the clouds looked like wads of white cotton.

Slowly, without realizing it, J.B. slid down onto his haunches. It would be so pleasant just to doze off. Just for a minute. His head slumped. The gun slid from his hand.

Miss Crandall allowed the horse to slow down to an easy lope when she believed she was far enough away that nobody would chase her. She was convinced that the third man had been coming down the canyon behind her and J.B., and would see his cohorts had climbed up and would follow them. Now that she felt safe, she had to allow the horse to slow down. No horse could run all the way to El Rey or even to the ranch, and running the horse to death would just leave her on foot and helpless. Besides, she had been accused of liking horses too much, and that was the truth.

When she saw the dim cattle trail, she remembered that the Diamond A had been running cattle up there a year earlier and had agreed to keep away now that Uncle Len had bought land up there. Was she on CC land now? If not, she was close. It occurred to her that one day they would have to fence the CC land; then she realized that the land was not theirs anymore. Well, she had no time to cry over that now.

J.B. was back there and probably facing two guns with his one pistol and only a few cartridges.

The cattle trail led off the mesa and down to the flats, and Miss Crandall was surprised to see how close she was to the CC Ranch buildings. It was a fairly easy trail, although at times the horse had to slow to a walk and pick its way carefully.

Then they were on the yucca flats, and she spurred the horse into a gallop again. The horse was tiring rapidly, and so was she. Sure, she had ridden bareback when she was a child, but not this far and not this fast. Every muscle in her body ached and her buttocks felt as if they were on fire. A saddle, any kind of a saddle, would have felt good right then.

How far now to El Rey? Too far. This horse will never make it.

No horse is made of iron. What I need is a fresh horse. Could I sneak into the ranch and steal one? Not likely. But come to think of it, maybe I can catch one out of the CC horse pasture. It's worth trying. I can skirt the ranch buildings and get to the horse pasture without being seen. There's that old bay I used to catch with a handful of oats. I don't have any oats, but maybe I can fool him. This horse can't go much farther. I've got to try. J.B. is up there with two men trying to kill him. I got him into this mess. I've got to get help.

She stayed out of sight of the ranch buildings and got to the horse pasture and through the barbwire gate without being seen. Most of the CC horses were scattered over the two-square-mile pasture. Where was the old bay? There he is. Just a little farther now.

She allowed the horse to slow to a walk when she got within two hundred yards of the bay. The old horse watched her approach. When she got within fifty feet of him, she slid off her mount, nearly collapsed, caught herself, straightened her knees painfully, and held out a hand.

"Whoa, Bobbie," she cooed. "Come here, will you?" Moving slowly, she took off her belt and put it folded in her hip pocket. "Here, Bobbie."

The old horse was not interested. She had fed him out of her hand many times, but not out in the open country. He watched her approach, then walked slowly away, ready to break into a run if necessary. He joined three other horses grazing nearby.

"Aw, Bobbie. If only you knew how badly I need you. Come on, Bobbie. Here, boy." The bay was not interested.

Frustration forced a sob into Miss Crandall's throat. "I can't ride a horse to death. But I have to. They'll kill J.B." She prepared to mount the weary horse again. "I'm sorry, old fella. I'm sorry."

Then she noticed that one of the other horses was watching her, ears pointed toward her. Where did that horse come from? Oh, that's that awkward-looking blue-roan J.B. was riding. What did J.B. call him? Amigo. "Here, Amigo. Here, boy. Whoa now."

The blue-roan allowed her to approach, then nuzzled her hand, expecting to find some grain. He allowed her to slip her belt around his neck, holding him captive. He stood quietly while she pulled the bridle off the hip-shot horse and put it on his head.

"Whoa, boy. Whoa, Amigo. Easy now." She stood beside the horse and tried to jump up on his back. "You're a tall old fella, aren't you? Boy, do I need those long legs of yours. Whoa now." She jumped again, got her chest over the horse's back, then scrambled astraddle. Her buttocks felt like one huge blister, and she let out a groan.

She got a hank of mane in her right hand to hang onto, then touched the horse with her spurs, "All right, Amigo, let's go to town." The blue-roan moved out into an easy, long-legged lope.

It was hoofbeats that awakened J.B. He immediately grabbed the gun and looked around. He stood up and looked over his fortress. It was a man on a horse, all right. It was Ed, the waddy. Now is when the ball begins, J.B. thought. J.B. drew a bead on the man's chest, but he knew the distance was too great for an accurate shot, and he sure as hell couldn't waste ammunition now.

How many shots did he have left? He tried to remember, to count each shot in his mind. He had only two left. Two enemies and two bullets. Well, as his older brothers told him when he was a kid, one bullet ought to bring home one rabbit.

In spite of his problems, a happy thought crossed J.B.'s mind: the girl had gotten past the third man. Miss Crandall was safe.

He saw Derby Hat stand up for a second and wave to get the third man's attention, then drop into his gulley again. The man dismounted and walked his horse to the gully, keeping the horse between him and J.B. Next, the man led his horse, still using the animal as a shield, farther away, out of gun range. J.B. could see only one man's hat and legs on the other side of the horse, and he guessed that Derby Hat had stayed put.

Six hundred yards away, the third man got on his horse and circled to J.B.'s left, over a rise and out of sight. Now what? What was that man going to do? Crawl back on his belly?

Pistol shots sounded, and J.B. knew Derby Hat was shooting at him. But of three shots fired, only one hit the outcropping and it wasn't even close enough to make J.B. blink. He guessed that Derby Hat had a cartridge belt full of ammunition and didn't mind wasting some of it. But why was he doing it? Trying to hold his attention while the other man did something sneaky? Another pistol bullet hit the rock and still another, that one closer. J.B. instinctively ducked.

When he heard the hoofbeats, he was surprised. He had to stand up and look over the rocks to see the third man riding hard toward him, firing a six-gun as he came. Was he crazy? Didn't he know he couldn't hit anything that way? J.B. watched him come, and when he was close enough, turned his pistol toward him, drew a bead on his chest, and...

Death missed J.B. by no more than an inch. The bullet hit the rock so close to his head that the sound of it deafened him for a moment, and rock fragments stung his face and neck.

"What the humped-up—?" he said aloud. He glanced from the man on the horse to the man in the gulley, and another bullet plucked at his shirt sleeve. It was Derby Hat shooting, and he had another rifle.

That was it. The waddy had given Derby Hat his rifle, and they had set up a trick. The man on the horse was to draw J.B.'s attention and his aim, and when J.B. exposed himself to take aim, Derby Hat was supposed to pick him off.

It damn near worked. It might work yet.

The horseman was bearing down on him, and for the second time, J.B. had to shoot a man out of the saddle or get shot. He had to shoot fast and he couldn't miss. He waited with his head down until the hoofbeats came within a hundred feet of him, then stood up quickly, got the front sight into the notch and on the horseman's chest, and squeezed the trigger. The gun boomed, and J.B. felt the recoil against his palm. He didn't wait to see whether he had hit or missed.

He dropped down immediately, and not a split second too soon. Derby Hat's rifle cracked, and a bullet chipped rock right where J.B.'s head had been.

The horse ran on by, and J.B. peered around the edge of the rock long enough to see that it was rider-less. The third man had to have been hit and was down.

Crawling on his hands and knees, J.B. peered around the other side of the rocks to his left. Yep, the man was lying on his side and not moving. "Good gawd amighty," J.B. said aloud, "he ain't more'n thirty feet away." The slight cowboy dragged a shirtsleeve across his eyes and sighed with relief. Two down and one to go. The gambler and the waddy had showed some recklessness, but Derby Hat didn't seem to be willing to take chances. All J.B. had to do now was wait him out.

One more bullet. He couldn't miss again. If he took another shot at Derby Hat, it had to be a good one. If he were in Derby Hat's place he'd try to draw another shot from J.B., then just walk over and pump rifle bullets into him. If I'm lucky, J.B. thought, he hasn't kept count. He don't know how bad off I am. Or he's scared to draw another shot from me.

At least I'm not sleepy anymore. That's good. I have to stay awake and watch 'im. Cain't let 'im sneak up. Watch 'im.

It wouldn't be long. The sun was close to the western horizon. J.B. peered over the rocks and saw Derby Hat's horse grazing not far from where the man was hiding. "I'd sure like to get to that horse," J.B. said, thinking out loud. "But he's got a better chance at him— when it gets dark, that is." The other horse had gone on down the country, dragging its bridle reins. It would be hard to catch.

"It'll happen this way," J.B. said, talking to himself again. "Ol' Derby Hat'll wait 'til it gits too dark to shoot straight, then he'll git on that horse and head for the CC headquarters. He'll git some help and he'll be back.

"It's gonna be a question of who gits back first, him or Miss Crandall. If she had to go clear to El Rey to git help, she won't be back 'til about noon. That is, if she rides most of the night. If he gits help at the ranch, he'll be back early in the mornin'. And they'll know exactly where to find me. I've got to move.

"One more ca'tridge. Wish I had more. Hell, come to think of it, I can git more. Soon's it gits dark. There's two dead men out there and both've got six-guns. While ol' Derby Hal is sneakin' away on his horse, I'll sneak me another gun."

J.B. knew he was safe as long as he kept an eye on the man in the gulley. He didn't dare show his head for more than a second, and he would have to take quick looks from different places behind the rocks to keep the man from getting him in his rifle sights. But he could do that.

He waited until the sun was sitting on the western horizon

before he took a longer look. The horse was still there, but it was on the other side of the gulley, where the man was hiding. It was getting farther away from J.B. all the time. The other horses were so far away there was no hope at all of catching them.

"Damn," the cowboy said aloud. "I ain't got a chance in the world of gettin' to that horse. Ol' Derby Hat's gonna git on 'im and go git some help."

Dusk arrived, and J.B. kept a closer watch on the gulley. He hoped the man would make his move while there was still enough light to shoot, but knew he wouldn't.

Slowly, the gulley and the landscape became obscured in the dark. The horse off in the distance became a vague shape. There was no movement in the gulley. Derby Hat was waiting until visibility was only a few yards. Maybe, J.B. thought, he'll wait until it's too dark to find that horse. Naw, he cain't be that dumb. Finally, J.B. figured it was safe to leave his fortress and help himself to the dead man's gun and belt. He started in that direction, and hadn't taken ten steps when he heard hoofbeats.

After listening for a couple of seconds, J.B. knew the hoofbeats were going away and his adversary was riding for reinforcements. It would take a few hours, but eventually, he would be back and J.B.'s life would be in very grave danger.

J.B. wondered what kind of odds a professional gambler would give. Probably, he thought with irony, that dead one over there and that rich one back in Santa Fe would bet ten to one that he wouldn't live another day. But then—J.B. grinned wryly in the dark—that dead one missed his bet when he made a target of himself and got shot.

"What I should've done," J.B. muttered, "was shoot that horse and put ol' Derby Hat afoot. But—aw, hell."

The nights of a full moon were over for a while, and the cowboy said under his breath, "It's darker than a stack of black cats." He kept walking, hobbling rather, to where he knew the dead man was. His shuffling walk paid off when he stumbled over the gun. He had its location fixed in his mind, but he might have missed it in the dark if he had not accidentally kicked it with his sore foot.

He picked it up, then continued walking until he stumbled over the body. This time he made sure it was his good foot and not the sore one that came into contact. Handling dead men was not the cowboy's favorite pastime, and he hesitated. He had never handled a dead man before. Then, with determination, he turned the body over on its back, unbuckled the gun belt, and pulled it free. He tried to buckle it around his own waist, but it was too large. He slid the gun into the holster and hung the belt over his shoulder.

After limping away from the body a few steps, J.B. stood in the dark and tried to decide what to do next. He had already decided he would have to move. Where? "Well, I cain't go nowhere in the dark," he said to himself. "Walkin' around on this canyon rim could git a man killed."

He went back to the outcropping, lay on his side with his arm under his head, and allowed himself to sleep.

It was not a sound sleep. His growling stomach kept him from sleeping well. Hunger, thirst, and the return of pain in his left foot and the side of his face awakened him just before dawn. He wished he were down in the canyon getting himself a drink out of the creek. A man could go a long time without food, but not so long without water. And he had to move anyway.

As soon as a dim light appeared on the eastern horizon, he got up and stood with his weight on the good foot. Shivering in the early-morning cold, he started hobbling back toward the spot where he and the girl had climbed out of the canyon. He tried not to look at the two dead men lying near the outcropping, and he veered around the body of the man in the batwing chaps. Looking around carefully, J.B. had hopes of seeing one of the loose horses. But they were not in sight. Walking was the best he could, or stay there where Derby Hat and company could easily find him.

By the time he got to the spot he was looking for, it was fully daylight, and by sliding and clawing for handholds, he made his way slowly and painfully down the steep hill. He cursed out loud when he started sliding uncontrollably and had to use his sore foot for a brake. Finally, he got to the bottom, and he hurried as fast as the blistered foot would allow to the creek, where he lay on his stomach and drank.

His thirst sated, he sat up, wiping his mouth with a shirt sleeve. The water was only a few degrees above freezing, and he hoped he could ease the dull burning in his left foot by dangling it in the water.

To do that, he would have to find a deeper hole than the shallow spot where he was.

With an eye on the creek edge, J.B. hobbled downstream until he found a place just behind a large boulder where the water was deep. He sat on a smaller boulder and tentatively put his foot in the water. A cold shock went through him and made him withdraw his foot immediately.

"Colder'n a witch's *culo*," he muttered. He forced himself to plunge his foot into the water.

He could stand it for only a few seconds, but it did make his foot feel better. If it relieved the pain in his foot, it ought to do his face some good too, he thought, and he stretched out, face down.

The water was so clear he could see his reflection in it. He could see his eyes, his hair moving slightly in the breeze, and his beard.

J.B. jerked his head back away from the water, his breath catching in his throat. That wasn't his face. He had no beard. For a long moment, he sat on the water's edge, his mind racing. No, he wasn't imagining things. That was a face. Somebody else's face. There was a man in the water.

Reluctantly, he peered into the pool again. The face was still there, its eyes wide open, staring, seeing nothing. A dead man's face. It was a dead man in the water.

Now that he was taking a careful look, J.B. could see that the body was half covered with sand washed over it by action of the creek. The slow movement of the water caused the hair to move as if waving in the wind. The man had a beard, brown or reddish brown. His hands were behind his back. He was barefoot, and his feet were tied together.

He was nobody that J.B. had ever seen before. And it was murder.

"Good gawd almighty." the cowboy said, drawing back. He sat on his haunches beside the creek. It couldn't be. Two dead men up there on the rim and another down here in the creek. Too many dead men. Where did this one come from? Who was he? Was J.B. imagining things? He looked around carefully, as if he half expected to find someone watching him. Leaning forward, he looked into the water. The man had been tied up and murdered, the way he and the girl had been tied. And his feet were bare, as if he had been tortured the way J.B. was tortured.

Had Derby Hat tortured this man too? And why? J.B. mulled that over in his mind—and suddenly he knew.

That explained it. That's why Derby Hat wanted him hung, and that's why Derby Hat stayed behind up there at the abandoned cabin. Derby Hat knew J.B. hadn't seen that money, and he had to have been the one who murdered the man in the creek. And the man in the creek had to be...

"Good gawd amighty," J.B. said aloud.

Men's voices brought his mind sharply back to the present. They came from up on the canyon rim. He didn't hear Miss Crandall. Derby Hat was back with reinforcements, and they were looking for J.B.

Best thing to do was to find another fortress, the cowboy decided, and keep out of sight the best he could in the meantime. He started to go downstream, looking for a likely pile of boulders, then got to thinking. He had climbed down from the rim not far from where he was standing, and they could do the same. Then he would have enemies behind him, and sooner or later others would get off the rim in front of him. He would be cornered. He had to go back upstream.

When he passed the spot where he had climbed down, he was exposed to the men above and they saw him. A shot followed a shout, and the bullet hit the ground only inches away.

Men yelled. "Git down there."

"Can't ride a hoss down. A hoss would have to slide down on his side."

"Go back a ways. We can get down there."

Sore foot or no sore foot, J.B. had to run. And run he did, grimacing with pain. Another shot was fired at him, but it missed by a good yard and a half. Half running and half hopping, J.B. kept going, until finally he was under a steep cliff and out of sight of the men on the rim.

He went another hundred yards before he came to two ton-sized boulders that had been shoved up together eons ago by rushing water.

J.B. climbed over them and looked back through the V between the two boulders. He could look back without exposing more than his head. This had to be the place to take his stand.

J.B. took cartridges from the pistol belt he had been carrying over his shoulder and filled the cylinder of the dead man's gun. He saw the bullets were .45's and he congratulated himself for bringing both weapons. One more shot and the gun he had taken from Derby Hat would be worthless.

Again he wished he had his hat. Somehow he felt more vulnerable without a hat. Aw, he thought grimly, what difference would it make? The last thing he needed to worry about was getting the top of his head sunburned. There were men with guns out there and he was their target. But until someone sneaked up on him from behind, he could hold them off pretty well. That is, if he didn't waste ammunition. How determined were those men? Derby Hat had them believing he'd killed Len Crandall and hidden his body and his money. They would want him, and some of them might be bold enough to risk their lives to get him. J.B. was in for another gunfight, no doubt about that. He grinned wryly when he thought about how he wouldn't even get to die with his boots on. Instead he'd die with one boot on. Well, he vowed, he'd go down fighting, not hanging.

It was a short wait. Three men on foot came around a bend in the narrow trail, moving cautiously, rifles in their hands. J.B. used the .45 and bounced a bullet off the rocks near the first man. The man, a short cowpuncher, stopped and turned back so suddenly he almost ran over the man behind him. They disappeared around the curve.

Long minutes passed. J.B. heard voices above, but he knew the men up on the rim couldn't see him. Their best strategy was to get behind him, and J.B. knew they would have to go only about three miles to get to a place behind him where they could ride down off the canyon rim. And that is what they would do. Sooner or later he would be caught in a cross fire.

He looked at the sky and saw that the sun hadn't climbed high enough yet that it could be seen from his position deep in the canyon. He guessed from the shadows on the western wall that it was about 10am. He calculated that Miss Crandall could be back about noon if she rode hard. Could she find help? The town people wouldn't harm her. They wanted J.B., not her. If she could talk to them, she could relate what Derby Hat and company had done, and the honest people would be outraged. They'd see that Derby Hat got his just deserts.

But that wouldn't get J.B. out of the stew. They would still believe he had killed Len Crandall and had hidden the CC Ranch's fortune. J.B. muttered, "You've done got yourself into a jackpot this time, Julian Bartholomew Watts."

More thoughts ran through his mind. Maybe the best thing to do was to surrender. He couldn't help thinking about it. Surely, they wouldn't hang him on the spot. They would take him to town and make a spectacle of it. It would give him some time. Given time, something could happen in his favor. His luck couldn't be all bad. He had Miss Crandall on his side, and the sheriff ought to be back by now.

If the sheriff had asked the right questions of the right people in Santa Fe, J.B. would no longer be suspected of murder. If the sheriff was back, he ought to be allowed to go on his way. "Yeah," he said to himself, "the smart thing to do is give up. That's the smart thing to do."

But then, there was the matter of stampeding a herd of cattle and nearly wiping out the main street of a town. They could hang him for that, or at least lock him up for a long, long time.

"Whoever said ol' J.B. Watts was smart," he said to himself.

The next man he saw was crawling on his stomach and elbows around the bend ahead. J.B. watched him, got him in his gunsights, but hesitated to shoot. The man wanted to see what the situation was, what kind of fortress their quarry was behind. He was a puncher, wearing leather chaps and spurs and a broad-brimmed hat. He was perhaps too eager to hang somebody, but he was doing what he thought was his duty.

Using the .45 again, J.B. fired another ricochet off the canyon's rock wall. The puncher had been crawling slowly forward. He suddenly took off, looking like a lizard running backwards.

More time had passed. They couldn't get to him from downstream and they had no doubt decided to wait until their companions got down onto the canyon bottom from upstream. The battle would be a short one after that. J.B. reached one definite decision: if he ever got ol' Derby Hat in his gunsights again, he would send ol' Derby Hat to his maker.

He couldn't fight off attackers from both directions at once, and his back wasn't too well hidden. Shaking his head sadly, J.B. wondered how much longer he had to live. Too bad. It was a hard life, but he had enjoyed it. The good times had offset the bad times. He had never given much thought to dying. Now he wondered what death was like.

J.B. was thinking thoughts like that when he heard voices again. Rather, it was a voice. He listened. Someone was calling his name. The angels? It sounded like an angel. Naw. He wasn't dead yet. Then what?

"J.B.," the voice yelled. "Don't shoot."

He listened intently.

"Don't shoot, J.B."

Suddenly he felt like shouting, not shooting. It was an angel. It was Miss Crandall. She was back.

"Hyo-o-o," he yelled, looking over the boulders. "It's me, J.B."

She appeared ahead of him, carrying a saddlebag, her blond hair shining in the sunlight. He stayed behind his fortress until she got there and climbed over one of the boulders. She sat on top of the boulder and smiled down at him. He grinned back.

For a moment, they smiled foolishly at each other. Then she reached into a saddlebag and handed him a small paper-wrapped package. "If you haven't forgotten how to eat," she said. "here's a steak sandwich." He took it. With unsteady hands, he unwrapped it and bit off a mouthful. He chewed hastily and swallowed. For a couple of seconds he thought he was going to be sick at his stomach.

"Take it easy, J.B.," she said. "A starving stomach has to be treated gently."

He ate slower, but still his stomach threatened to hand it back up to him. She watched him, smiling, until he got half the sandwich down. "Save the rest. In about an hour you can eat it with no difficulty."

He wiped his mouth with a shirt sleeve and tried to grin at her, but his heaving stomach wiped any semblance of a grin off his face.

She nodded back the way she had come. "They didn't know it,

but if they had waited a little longer, you would have died of natural causes. Darned if you aren't the sorriest-looking specimen I have ever had the misfortune of coming face to face with." She continued smiling to show she was only kidding. "You ought to see yourself. You've got a week's growth of whiskers, blond ones too, your hair is standing out in all directions, your face is blistered, your eyebrows and the hair on the front of your head is singed, your nose is sunburned and peeling, and your shirttail is out."

He could only stare at her with a sick feeling in his stomach. She continued, "I do believe the only humane thing to do is to shoot you and put you out of your misery."

The sick feeling subsided a bit and he managed a crooked grin. "I can still whup you and all your relations."

"Can you sit on a horse, or have you grown fond of walking?"

"If you've got an extra horse and can get us past those men, I'll set on 'im or hang on 'im."

Another figure came around the curve then, and J.B. tensed, gripping the pistol. She looked back and yelled, "Come on, he's halter broke now." To J.B., she said, "Don't worry. That's Sheriff White. He's still not convinced you're innocent, but he promised you won't be hung until you get a fair trial."

"A fair trial," J.B. said glumly. "I'm right back where I started, huh?"

"Not by a long shot. He still hasn't found Uncle Len's whereabouts, and as he put it, 'You can't prove murder without a corpus delicti.' Besides, after what happened to you and me, the town has a lot more to think about than hanging you."

"Oh, Lord," J.B. groaned, seeing visions of a dead man in the creek.

"Are you going to throw up?"

"It's not my stomach, it's, uh..."

"What?"

CHAPTER 10

The sheriff arrived then, walked around the boulders, and held his hand out to J.B. At first the cowboy wondered if the sheriff wanted to shake hands, but on second thought, that wasn't likely.

"Give me your guns," the sheriff ordered, his bushy eyebrows waving like the antenna on a cockroach. J.B. glanced at Miss Crandall and back at the sheriff.

"Let him have them," she said. "He has promised me you won't have to defend yourself again."

"You are innocent until proven guilty," Sheriff White said, "and you have protection under the law."

"If that's right," said J.B., "why in hell—excuse me, Miss Crandall—why in hell was I locked up in your jail?"

"You were taken into protective custody," the sheriff said, as if reciting from memory. "You are in custody now."

"So I'm still under arrest?"

Miss Crandall cleared her throat to get J.B.'s attention, then winked at him. "You'll be a guest of the county, but only for tonight, J.B." She winked again.

J.B. handed over his guns. The sheriff yelled for someone to bring the horses. Five men gathered around J.B., and their faces were not friendly. Derby Hat was not among them.

The cowboy asked if they had found the two bodies on top of the rim, and the sheriff said they had and he was satisfied that their deaths were self-defense.

"Where is he?" J.B. asked. "Who?" the sheriff said. "The man in the Derby Hat."

"Oh, Dutch Schultz? He went on back to the CC Ranch. He won't go far."

Three riders came from upstream then, their horses splashing across the creek, their guns drawn. When they recognized the sheriff, they holstered their guns. When a horse was led up to J.B., he started to put his injured foot into a stirrup, then stopped. An unpleasant memory crossed his mind and he looked over at Miss Crandall.

"Uh, Miss Crandall, what did—does—your uncle look like?"

"Why?" Her eyes narrowed.

He shrugged, trying to act as if the question were not important. "I wondered if I might have seen him somewhere."

She was not fooled. "Why do you ask, J.B.?"

"What does he look like? Does he have a beard, either brown or reddish?"

She turned a little pale. "He does. Have you seen him?"

He hated to tell her, but he had to. "Yeah. I think I know where his body is."

He led them to the pool. Three men reached into the bitterly cold water and lifted the body out. They laid it on the trail. Hats were removed, and the men stood bareheaded in reverence to the dead. "It's Len Crandall," someone said in a hushed tone.

Miss Crandall stood over the body, her head bowed. A tear ran slowly down her cheek and dripped off her chin. J.B. wanted to touch her, put his arms around her. But he didn't know whether she would appreciate that. She turned to the sheriff, her face strained. "What did they do to him? Look at him. His feet. Did they torture him the way they did J.B.?"

"Shore looks that way," a puncher allowed.

She knelt beside the body and tenderly touched the face. She stood up and walked down the trail a short distance away from the men, her back to them. They stood silently, hats in their hands, until she was ready to rejoin them.

Because they had no extra horses, the sheriff left two temporary deputies with the body, promising to send someone back with a pack horse. "I hope he gets back before dark," a deputy said. "I don't like campin' with a dead man."

The ride to El Rey was a quiet one. J.B. finished the sandwich as he rode and was happy to find that his stomach kept it down. They rode single file until they got out of the canyon and into the rocky foothills. Miss Crandall sat on her saddle sorely and rode her stirrups as much as possible. J.B. noticed that.

A quarter mile from the bottom of the canyon, J.B. could see the CC Ranch headquarters. He could see where the creek, full of rain runoff, splashed its way past the buildings, and farther along, he could see where water from the creek had been used to irrigate a vega, what Miss Crandall had called a meadow. Grass was stirrup high on the vega and was ready to be cut, raked and stacked. The girl was right. Whoever had homesteaded that country knew exactly what they were doing. They had one of the best small ranches he had ever seen. Not only that, without court-established water rights, owners of the ranch controlled most of the water downstream too. Bloody battles had been fought over water. No wonder the bank was so quick to foreclose. With that piece of property, the bank owners could dictate to every landowner from the foot of Juniper Creek to where Juniper Creek joined the Canadian River. And that was a hell of a lot of territory.

When they topped the hill on the west of El Rey, J.B. could see that the railroad pens were empty, and that the town had been partially rebuilt. There were still some sagging roofs and broken windows, but the town appeared to be going on about its business.

Miss Crandall grinned wryly when she told him about the longhorns being rounded up over the past two days and loaded on rail cars early that morning. "The Box O was secretly glad you stampeded their beeves," she said. "That gave them an excuse to graze them on someone else's grass until shipping time. But of course they wouldn't admit that in a million years."

"The Box O is the outfit owned by the bank, is it?" J.B. asked.

"Yes. By Mr. Buetel and the bank."

"And most of their country is downstream from the CC?"

"Right again, J.B., and what you're thinking is correct too. Until a couple of days ago, we could have forced the Box O to dig wells and try to pump water to their stock. We didn't, but Uncle Len was threatening to."

"Uh huh," said J.B.

She studied his face. "You've got some ideas going around in your head, haven't you? And this time, I'm not sure what you're thinking."

"I'm not sure either," he said.

Townspeople turned and stared as the group rode past and up to the sheriff's office. A small crowd gathered as they dismounted. Included in the crowd was the woman with the stringy hair and the gap in her teeth. "That's him," she shrieked. "That's the *chinqadero* that did it."

The crowd had angry faces, but no one made a threatening move toward the prisoner. Once inside the adobe building, the sheriff dropped wearily into a wooden chair behind his desk, put his feet up, shoved his hat back, and said, "Just set right there, young feller, and tell me everything that happened." He nodded toward one of three chairs scattered around the small room. J.B. sat.

The girl answered for him. "I've already told you everything that happened."

"I want to hear him tell it. There's two dead men up there on that mesa, and I've got to make out a formal report to the territorial marshal."

"I told you how one of them died, and I can make a good guess as to how the other got shot."

The sheriff's feet came down and he scowled at her. "Now, Miss Crandall, I want—"

She cut him off. "This man has been through a terrible ordeal. He has been tortured and is in pain from his wounds. He is half starved and half dead from the lack of rest. You give him some food and rest or I'll be communicating with the territorial marshal myself."

Sheriff White thought that over. "Well, I guess it don't matter when I get the information from him."

"And get him some salve for those blisters," she ordered. "And get him some blankets for that bunk in there."

J.B. slumped in his chair. "So I'm gonna be locked up again, huh?"

"Only until tomorrow," she answered. "Judge Wilson will be here tomorrow on the train, and he and my father and mother were good friends. If he says to turn you loose, the sheriff will turn you loose."

"Jail's the safest place for you tonight anyhow," the sheriff put in. "There's folks in this town that'd like to hang you just for stampedin' them cattle."

Weariness forced a yawn out of the cowboy. He was having a hard time keeping his eyes open. The pain in his left foot was forgotten for the moment. "Well," he said drowsily, "any bed'd look mighty good right now, but there's lots of places I'd rather sleep than in a jail."

Jail or no jail, he slept. A deputy produced two wool blankets and even a pillow for the bunk. J.B. fell onto it and passed out. His sleep was troubled at first. In his dreams he was reminded that he had killed two men and a horse. He had never killed a man or a horse before. Somehow, the dead horse haunted him more than the dead men. But then his dreams turned very pleasant. He dreamed that a fair-haired angel appeared in the cell with him and was spreading a soothing salve over his blistered foot and face. She cooed to him and told him everything was going to be fine, and her hand and the salve felt wonderful. A smile spread over his face. When she quietly left, J.B. slept like a dead man.

When Miss Crandall left the jail, she went back to the town's one hotel, a two-story clapboard building, wearily climbed the stairs, went to her room, and undressed slowly and painfully. She applied some of the salve to the part of her anatomy that was inflamed from a long, fast ride on bareback horses. That done, she fell across the bed and dropped immediately into a deep sleep. Later that night, she awakened long enough to crawl between the blankets. She slept until sunrise the next morning.

A deputy that morning brought J.B. a wash basin of warm water, a razor, and a mirror. The cowboy grimaced when he saw his reflection. His face was red and blistered, and his eyebrows and the hair on the front of his head were fuzzy. He almost didn't recognize himself. He shaved gingerly and missed a few hairs that grew out of the blisters.

The same deputy brought him breakfast: eggs, bacon, hot cakes, syrup, and black coffee in a chipped china mug. The deputy was the lanky one who talked with a painfully slow drawl. He stood in the open cell door and watched the prisoner dig into it. "You've had a purty rough time of it, ain't you, cowboy?"

"Uh huh," J.B. said as he forked food into his mouth. His stomach was complaining a little, but only a little.

"Well, I don't think you done any wrong," he drawled, "except maybe stampede them beeves."

J.B.'s eyebrows, what was left of them, went up, but he continued chewing rapidly.

"We found that sorrel horse," the deputy went on. "The one that Len Crandall was ridin'. Red Feather, they called 'im."

"What?" J.B. stopped chewing then.

"A cowman comin' back from Raton found 'im. Saw some satchel birds—you know, magpies—gatherin' and went for a look see. The horse was dead. Shot."

"When?"

"Yestiddy. Same time the shurff was goin' after you. I was here alone when the cowman told about it. I didn't git a chance to tell the shurff 'til last night."

"Comin' from Raton, you say?"

"Yep."

"I came from Santa Fe."

"I know you did. I went down there with the shurff and found a bartender that remembered seein' a puncher that looks like you. Remembered somebody callin' you J.B. You couldn't've rode that far north at the time ol' Len Crandall was seen last.'

"Does the sheriff know all this?"

"Knows now. I told 'im. He'll be lettin' you out purty soon."

J.B. put the plate of food aside. "How long is it gonna take 'im to git around to it?"

"Eat your breakfast," the deputy advised. "It's free." He turned to go, then looked back. "And I don't blame you much for stampedin' them Box O cattle neither." He grinned. "That was some ee-vent."

When he left, J.B. picked up the plate and finished his meal. Miss Crandall was his next visitor. She was wearing clean denims and another blue checkered shirt. Her blond hair had been combed until it shone, and her face was cheerful.

"Joel came to see me while I was eating breakfast," she said. "He went back up that canyon to get your saddle, and he said he'd bring a pair of his old boots for you. His feet are bigger than yours, so maybe you can get the left one on over your sore foot. Here." She handed him a glass jar a quarter full of white salve. "I bought it at the store last night. It helps, I can tell you that, and it can't do any harm. My, you look better this morning. How do you feel?"

He grinned. "Finer'n the fur on a cat's back. What I want now is to git out of here."

"Well, you just wait one minute." She left and was gone two minutes. When she came back, the deputy was with her. He unlocked the cell door and swung it wide.

"Shurff said to let you out. He had to go out to the Box O outfit. 'Nother dead man."

"Who now?" the girl asked.

"Feller said it was Dutch Schultz."

"The man with the derby hat?"

"Yep. That's him."

"How?"

"Shot. In the back. Feller found 'im 'bout halfway twixt here and the ranch house."

J.B. wanted to know immediately if the killer had been identified, but the girl beat him to the question. "Who shot him?"

"Don't know. Looks like 'nother mystery."

The girl and J.B. looked at each other, question marks on their faces.

"The mystery deepens," the girl said.

"That do beat all," said J.B.

Still limping and with one foot bare, J.B. went out into the sunlight, the girl beside him. He squinted at the sun, and allowed it was good to be out with nobody chasing him.

"I took the liberty of renting you a room at the hotel," she said. "You still need rest."

"What I need is my boot and my hat and my horse and my outfit," he said.

A frown wrinkle appeared between her blue eyes. "You're not going to ride out now, are you, J.B.?"

He mulled it over in his mind before he answered. "No. Not if you don't want me to. You've still got troubles, and I never quit a friend in trouble yet, and I'm too old to start now."

She smiled and took his left arm to help him walk. "I do need your help, cowboy. There is no one in the whole wide world I would rather have on my side."

"What do you think we ought to do next?"

"Next? Well, next, we are going to get you a new hat."

"With what? My good looks?"

"With my money. Your looks wouldn't buy a sack of tobacco right now."

"You're a gal with money?"

"Sure. Uncle Len didn't take all the money in the house, and I've got the gold you found. And I owe you, so don't worry about getting a present from a woman."

"I'm worried about it, but I'm worried even more about goin' bareheaded."

The roof of the town's one store was sagging, and a workman with a hammer and saw was trying to repair it. He stopped what he was doing and stared hard at J.B. and the girl as they went past and into the building.

The storekeeper, a bald man with half-lens glasses on the end of his nose and an apron around his middle, also stared. He scowled. "You're not...? You're the one that—"

"Yes he is," the girl snapped. "What would you have done, Mr. Ryan? This town wanted to hang him for a crime he knew nothing about. He had a right to his revenge. And," she smiled, "boy, did he get it."

His scowl faded slowly, and he shrugged. "Oh, well, what can I sell you, Miss Crandall?"

They found a black, broad-brimmed hat much like the one J.B. had lost. It was an eighth of a size too large, but by putting folded paper inside the sweatband it fit pretty well. J.B. asked for a length of string too, then left the store carrying the hat instead of wearing it. He hobbled to the livery stable with the girl beside him.

There, he shoved the hat under water in a wooden trough until it was thoroughly wet. Then he curled the brim and creased the top down low, squared the front and back Texas style, and tied the whole thing in place with the string.

The girl, wise to the ways of cowboys, knew what he was doing and asked no questions. "It won't take very long to dry," she said. "Tell you what. While it's drying and you are taking a long hot bath at the hotel, I'll get you some new Levi's and a shirt. If you'll tell me what size you wear."

"Now just a doggone minute, Miss Crandall. Shine. You cain't be buyin' me stuff like that."

Her face took on that determined look. "I owe it to you. Besides"—she dug into her pocket and pulled out some gold coins—"if it weren't for you, I wouldn't have these."

He knew arguing would be a waste of time.

The hotel clerk said he had already built a fire under the water tank and that it would heat quickly. J.B. went up to room 104 and placed the new hat with the string around it carefully on the bed. The girl followed him into the room.

"I had my bath this morning," she said, "and it was wonderful. Now there's a towel and a bar of soap, and when you get back up here, I'll have some new clothes for you." She left.

J.B. picked up the towel and soap and went downstairs to the bathroom. The hotel had only two, one for men and one for ladies. The tub in the men's room was made of galvanized steel and looked more like a small stock tank than a bathtub. A spigot poked through a wooden wall from a tank in the next room. The cowboy turned the spigot, and warm water poured out. He undressed and got gingerly into the tub. The water was exactly the right temperature, and he soon relaxed, leaned back, and let it soak some of the soreness and weariness out of his body. He dozed in that position until the water turned cool, then he lathered himself from head to foot and washed thoroughly. He rinsed by ducking under the water. Then he stood up and reached for the towel.

"Hey, are you still alive in there?" It was the girl, and J.B., knowing how bold she was, would not have been surprised to see her barging through the door. He grabbed the towel quickly and wrapped it around his waist.

"Don't come in here," he said.

"Don't worry. But can I open the door and put these clothes inside?"

"No."

"You don't want to put on dirty clothes, do you?"

"Yeah."

A pause, then, "Oh, all right. I'll leave them in your room."

J.B. put on his dirty pants and a shirt and walked barefoot, carrying his one boot and sock, upstairs to his room. New pants, a pale blue shirt, and a pair of socks were laid out on the bed. There was even a pair of broadcloth shorts, a shade too large but wearable. He hastily stripped off the dirty clothes and put on the shirt, buttoned it, then the shorts and the new Levi's denim pants. The shirt was made of some kind of silky material, the likes of which J.B. had never worn before. He sat on the bed and put on the right sock, then tried the left one. He noticed with satisfaction that the blisters on his left foot had been reduced somewhat, even though the foot was still sore.

But by rolling up the sock and placing it on his toes, then unrolling it up his foot ever so carefully, he got it on. He stood up and put his weight on the foot. Yep, it was better. At least he wouldn't have to go around with one bare foot now.

The room contained the bed, a dresser with a long mirror, a wash basin, and a wooden chair. J.B. studied himself in the mirror and didn't like what he saw. Besides the blistered face and singed hair, there was the new Levi's. Cut large in the legs to allow for shrinkage, the denims stood out at the sides like a pair of English riding breeches. J.B. hated the looks of brand new unshrunk denims, and always before, when he bought a pair, he soaked them in a stock tank and hung them up to dry before wearing them.

When the knock on the door came, J.B. opened it, expecting to find Miss Crandall there. Instead, he found Sheriff White and the lanky deputy. "I still have to get a statement from you," the sheriff said. "And I have to get it before you leave town."

"I'm not leavin' for a while, sheriff."

"You're not?" The lawman seemed surprised.

"No."

The lawman looked at his deputy and back at J.B. "There's folks here that want you locked up again or out of town. You did a lot of damage to property here, and they don't want you to get away with it. The circuit judge is in town now, and he'll give you thirty days for what you done."

J.B. held the sheriff's gaze a moment. "So I git out of town or spend the next thirty days in jail, is that it?"

"That's it, young feller. I'm givin' you a break."

"Who wants me out of town?"

"Everybody."

"Name some of 'em."

Holding up one hand, the sheriff began counting on his fingers. "Well, there's Red Garrett that owns the Red Dog saloon, there's Ben Adams, foreman of the Box O that had to gather up them cattle you run off, and there's John Buetel, president of the bank that had its front door busted up."

"John Buetel?" J.B. asked. "Ain't he owner of the Box O?"

"Yes, he is."

"And the foreman of the Box O works for him and would do anything John Buetel tells 'im to." It was a statement, not a question.

The sheriff nodded in agreement.

"I'll bet," J.B. said, face screwed up in thought, "that bank holds a mortgage on the saloon, too. Say," he said, face brightening, "how about the store? Does Buetel hold a mortgage on that too?"

"No, I don't believe he does. Old Ryan came down here from Colorado and built that store hisself."

"Did Mr. Ryan say he wanted me locked up or run off? His store was damaged too."

"No-o-o," Sheriff White said, pondering the question. "No, he told me he hoped the town learned a lesson and he wouldn't make a complaint."

J.B. let that sink in, then: "Tell me somethin', sheriff, what was ol' Buetel doin' out with you and your deputies the day you first saw me? I mean, him bein' a banker and all, how come he was ridin' with the law?"

"You're askin' a lot of questions, young feller, and they're questions that don't concern you."

"I spent some time in your jail because a man disappeared, and I've got a right to know what happened to 'im."

The sheriff scratched his nearly bald head, then yanked his hat down hard. "You just come on over to the office with me. I'm the law around here and I ask all the questions."

J.B. believed it useless to pump the sheriff for more information. He stepped back into the room, picked up the new hat, saw it was still damp, left it, and followed the sheriff and the deputy. As he limped sorely down the stairs, he muttered, "I knew there had to be a reason I never liked lawmen."

"What did you say, young feller?"

"Aw, nothin'."

CHAPTER 11

It was afternoon when he finished telling about what happened from the time of the stampede until the sheriff and Miss Crandall found him on the Juniper Canyon trail. The sheriff shook his head negatively when he told about the shooting, but smiled briefly when he told about how Miss Crandall risked her life going for help.

"There's a young lady with more nerve than any two men I've ever met," he said. Then his bushy eyebrows came together again. "But you've killed two men, and I don't cotton to drifters comin' around here and killin' folks."

"It don't matter that they would've killed me and the young lady too, does it?"

"Of course it matters. If it didn't, you'd be right back in that cell waitin' trial for murder. Now I'm offerin' you another chance to get out of town before some prominent citizens insist on your arrest."

"Prominent citizens," J.B. muttered, half under his breath, as he stood up.

"What did you say, young feller?"

"Aw, nothin'."

The left foot was treated gently as J.B. walked back toward the hotel. He was met on the plank sidewalk by Miss Crandall. He told her about the sheriff's ultimatum and said he couldn't argue with the law even though the law was sometimes unfair. She mulled it over in her mind, then had to agree that perhaps it would save a lot of trouble if he did make himself scarce for the time being. But she insisted that they eat first in the town's one restaurant, and wait for Joel to return with J.B.'s saddle. She told him about catching his blue-roan horse and riding him the rest of the way to town, and how the horse was resting and eating good hay now in a feedlot at the livery barn.

J.B. had to chuckle. "He's a good traveler, but as skinny as he is, I'd hate to ride 'im bareback."

The girl winced at the thought, but said, "I'll always be grateful to him for letting me catch him."

Shaking his head, J.B. said, "That ol' pony sure don't owe nobody anything."

"Well, anyway, cowboy, let's get inside Winters' Cafe and get outside some food."

"Had a good breakfast, though it didn't make up for all the meals I've missed the last three or four days,"

J.B. allowed. "But," he added sourly, "I still ain't got two nickels to rub together, and I've never lived off a woman in my life."

"Here." She handed him two gold coins. "Back east, when a person finds lost money, he or she gets ten percent. There were twenty double eagles in that pouch."

He handed them back. "We ain't back east and I don't take money for doin' nothin'. But I will let you buy me a meal. I'll pay you back whenever I can."

Winters' Cafe had a false front, as did most of the buildings on El Rey's main street. Inside, the restaurant was clean and neat, with a half-dozen handmade wooden tables surrounded by handmade wooden chairs. The tables were covered with red checkered oilcloth. Only two of the tables were occupied when J.B. and Miss Crandall entered. They were stared at but not bothered.

Their waitress was a pretty dark-haired, dark-eyed young lady who hurried from behind a wooden counter to serve them. Recognition showed in Miss Crandall's eyes, and she said, "You're Margaret, aren't you?"

"Yes, Miss Crandall."

Holding out her right hand, Miss Crandall said, "I'm so happy to meet you. Joel told us about you, and I just know the two of you are going to make a wonderful couple."

They shook hands briefly. "I'm sorry about the ranch, Miss

Crandall. Joel feels like it's his loss too. I wish there was something we could do. We'd do anything."

A frown crossed Miss Crandall's face, but only for a second, then she smiled. "Don't give up. I haven't." She touched J.B.'s shoulder. "We're not finished yet."

They ordered steak with fried potatoes, sourdough biscuits, and pan gravy. As was the custom with ranch folk, they ate the meal in silence. Finished, they washed it down with strong black coffee. J.B. had just drained his cup when Joel came in.

The tall, broad-shouldered cowboy eased his slender hips into a chair beside Miss Crandall. He took off his hat and placed it on the floor beside his chair. His face was burned a dark brown from the eyebrows down, but was lily-white from the eyebrows up, where it was nearly always covered with a hat. He had dark, curly hair. J.B. guessed he could be a lady killer when he wanted to be.

"I got your saddle," he said to J.B. "Took it over to the livery barn where your blue-roan hawrse is."

"I sure do thank you, Joel," J.B. said. "Hope I can do you a good turn sometime."

"*Por nada*," the tall man said. He turned to the girl. "What're you gonna do now, Miss Crandall?"

"I can't leave now, Joel. Uncle Len was tortured and murdered, and I want to know who did it."

"Got any hunches?" Joel asked.

"None at the moment," she said. "Have you, J.B.?"

While J.B. was mulling over an answer, the waitress, Margaret, came over and stood beside Joel. The tall cowboy stood up and put a possessive arm around her waist. J.B. glanced around the room at the five other customers, leaned forward, ready to answer Miss Crandall's question in a low voice. He stopped without saying anything when Joel suddenly reached for his hat on the floor and prepared to leave. John Buetel had just come in the door.

Joel was nervous. "Howdy, Mr. Buetel," he said.

The bull-necked banker frowned. "What are you doing here, Joel?"

"I had to return a saddle, Mr. Buetel," he answered uncertainly.

Buetel shrugged and, without asking whose saddle, said, "You can't get any work done in here." He dismissed his foreman, sat at a table, and studied the three-item menu that had been written by hand on a sheet of plain paper.

Joel smiled weakly at Miss Crandall. "I got to go," he said, "but if you need my help for anything, just whistle."

She returned his smile. "I'll do that, Joel, and thanks."

He left, the large rowels of his spurs dragging on the floor.

"Here." She shoved a gold coin at J.B. "You pay the bill."

"No, I cain't," he said. "It's your money."

"But," she said, puzzled, "I thought you'd want to, for appearance's sake."

"No, I ain't puttin' on any phony act."

"You never cease to amaze me, cowboy."

It was awkward, walking with a high-heeled boot on one foot and nothing but a sock on the other, and J.B. still hadn't gotten used to it. He felt as if he were lopsided and going sideways. He found his saddle at the livery barn, and tied to it was a boot for the left foot. J.B. leaned against the barn wall and tried the boot on. It was large enough that he got it on over the blisters. That was better. His left foot was still sore, but now he at least could walk straight.

The girl dickered with the stableman, who fetched the blue-roan from a feedlot next to the barn. "Now," said J.B., "I got to git my hat and I'll be ready to ride."

"I'll get a horse and go with you, J.B. I'll meet you here in a half hour. All right?"

"Why, Miss Crandall?"

"The name is Shine, understand? Why? Because we're still working together, aren't we?"

"Well, sure, but where're we goin'?"

"We're not leaving the country, you can tell the whole wide world that. We'll have to think of something."

The hat was still a little damp, but it had dried enough that it retained the shape he had designed. He put it on, and knew that when it dried completely, it would fit his head perfectly and stay on in the strongest winds. A cowboy almost never lost his hat.

Miss Crandall had saddle bags and a canvas-wrapped sleeping bag rolled tightly and tied behind her saddle. When J.B. asked about it, she answered, "You can't come back to town without danger of being arrested, and if you have to camp out, I'm going to camp out with you."

"But," he protested, "you cain't camp out with me. You don't have to stay out of town."

"I can't?" Her eyebrows went up and that half smile played around the corners of her mouth again.

J.B. shrugged, mounted, and headed west out of town. She rode beside him. "Besides," she said, pointing to the saddlebags, "I've got all the grub."

They rode over the hill beside the railroad pens and out of town with little conversation. J.B. was deep in thought. Finally, he asked, "I told you I'd do what I can to help you. But where're we goin'? And what're we gonna do?"

"We're going money hunting," she said.

"Any idea where to hunt?"

"Look." She half turned in her saddle toward J.B. "Someone shot Uncle Len's horse from under him, took him at gunpoint up to that line camp, and tortured him." She let those words sink in, then added, "Now, why would they torture him?"

J.B. snorted. "I'm a dumb cowpuncher, Shine, but even I had that idea."

"And you were right. They tortured him because he managed somehow to hide the money."

He nodded in agreement.

"So," she said, "how do you think he managed to do it?"

"Now that," he said, "is somethin' a dumb cowpuncher cain't figure out."

"What's your best guess?"

"I've been thinkin' about it," J.B. said, "and I just don't know. I'm hopin' we can find the spot where he first saw somebody after 'im and took off, tryin' to ride away from 'em. Seems to me if we can find the trail they made, we can find out where he dumped the money."

She smiled at him. "You're brilliant. That's a terrific idea. Only

126

one thing wrong."

"Yeah, I know. Whoever chased 'im knows he had to've dumped those saddlebags before they caught up with 'im, and they know where they chased 'im. If that money was easy to find, they would've found it."

"Correct. And of course there's another possibility."

"Yeah, I know that too. They could've forced him to tell where he dumped it. Whoever it was might have the money right now."

"Correct again. But I don't think so."

"You don't?"

"No. I know—knew—Uncle Len. He was the stubbornest man I have ever known. He was, uh, eccentric, as I said, and I don't think anyone could force him to do anything he didn't want to do."

"Uh, huh," the cowboy said, "and if that's the case..." He looked behind them, saw nobody. "If that's the case..."

"What, J.B.? What are you thinking?"

"I was just thinkin' that we ain't the only ones looking for that money."

This time she was surprised. "You're right. What this means is, if we see someone else looking, we'll know who the murderers are."

"Yeah, and us with no guns."

"Wrong." She reached back into one of the saddlebags. "Here." She handed J.B. a six-gun, a .45 Colt.

He took it and checked the cylinder. It was fully loaded. She next handed him a box of cartridges.

"Forty-fives," he said, "Where'd you git 'em?"

"Stole them. Out of the sheriff's office."

He grinned at her. "If I'm ever missin' anything, I'll know where to look."

"Necessity breeds criminals," she said, smiling.

They rode in silence a mile, allowing their horses to walk. Then J.B. said, looking straight ahead, "I'm just a dumb cowpuncher, Shine, but I was a step ahead of you."

"You're not dumb, J.B., and I wouldn't be surprised if you were two steps ahead of me."

Silence.

"Well, are you going to tell me?"

"Tell you what?"

Exasperation tore the words out of her mouth. "J.B., if you don't tell me what you're thinking, I'll pull you out of that saddle and punch you in the nose."

He grinned. "You and whose army?"

"J.B.!" Her tone was threatening.

"All right. Look at it this way, Shine. We both know who killed your uncle, don't we? I mean, we know Dutch Schultz was one of the killers."

"Oh, that. I was wondering if you'd mention it or if I would have to."

"Yeah, but knowin' that makes it plain he didn't find the money."

"How's that?"

"'Cause he wouldn't't've been so anxious to catch us and torture us too."

"You're absolutely right. And I have to admit I hadn't thought of that. And now that you mention it, I wondered at the time why he was so accommodating to his cohorts at the line camp, the cabin. I mean, volunteering to stay behind and guard us."

"Sure. He knew I was makin' up a story."

"But now he's dead. Shot in the back, someone said. And J.B." She paused before continuing. "You keep talking as if there were more than one killer."

"There was."

"Who else?"

"You just said yourself there was 'murderers' 'stead of 'murderer'."

"Do you know who else besides Dutch Schultz?"

"Maybe." He touched his boot heels to the blue-roan's sides, and the horse moved into a fast trot.

"We've got a lot of ridin' to do."

She lifted her horse into a gallop and caught up with him. "Who else, J.B.?" She yelled at him as the breeze ruffled her shoulder length blond hair. "I'm going to punch you, J.B."

It was near dark when they rode into the ravine where J.B. had found the rain slicker and pouch of gold. The girl estimated they were four miles from the CC Ranch headquarters and ten miles from town. They knew they could do no tracking in the dark, and there was no fuel for a fire at the ravine, so they traveled another mile to the foothills where there was piñon and scrub pine, and where bunch grass for the horses was plentiful. They also found a small stream of water in a stream bed that was normally dry.

After unsaddling and hobbling the horses, they gathered firewood. J.B. used his pocket knife to cut a small pile of splinters, then got a fire started. He took the bed tarp off his saddle, laid it on the ground, and folded one half its fourteen-foot length back over the other half. Normally, he would have had some blankets to spread between the halves to make a bed, but this time he had none.

The girl took the sleeping bag off her saddle and unrolled it on the other side of the fire. It was about six feet long and barely wide enough for a small human to fit into. Buttons made of plaited rawhide held it together.

They used green branches to warm the cooked steaks she'd brought. They were delicious, and with a couple of sourdough biscuits, the meal was filling.

It was dark then, and it seemed as if their whole world consisted of that one little circle of firelight.

"That's the kind of chuck that'll take the wrinkles out," J.B. said.

"I brought enough for tomorrow," she said. She got up and went to the creek for a drink, then returned to the other side of the fire. Her face screwed up in pain for a second when she sat down again on the hard ground.

"I know the feelin'," J.B. said sympathetically. "I've lived on horses' backs for a good many years, but it'd kill me to ride bareback that far. 'Specially on that Ol' Amigo horse of mine."

That slow, half-smile turned up the corners of her mouth, and then she chuckled. "It kind of makes us even, doesn't it, J.B.?"

He had to chuckle with her. "Yeah, we've both got blisters. Me on the foot and you on the—"

"J.B.!" she screeched, laughing.

The cowboy wanted to continue the joke, but he could think of no way to do it without becoming too personal. He believed she would not appreciate that.

When their laughter subsided, he rolled a cigarette. Then they talked about more serious matters.

"Your uncle had to've been headed for El Rey," J.B. allowed, "or he wouldn't've rode down in that 'royo. That's south of the road. But his horse was found north of here, on the way to Raton. How?"

"I've been wondering about that too, the girl said. "The only possible answer is he saw them ahead on the road to El Rey, knew what they were after, and ran them a race, going south to the arroyo, then doubling back to the north."

J.B. stared into the fire, then said, "I just cain't figure out why he dumped his slicker and poke of gold down there. It was a lot of money but you say not enough to pay off the mortgage."

"I don't understand it either," she said, also staring into the fire. "As a matter of fact, I don't understand why he was carrying the poke, as you call it, separate from the rest of his money."

J.B. reached for the small pile of firewood they'd gathered and tossed another piece onto the flames. The wood was damp, and it sizzled for a moment before catching fire.

"It sure is a puzzler," he said. "Do you know this country good enough to find the spot where his dead horse is?"

"Yes, I got a good enough description of it that I can find it. Why?"

"Well, he rode there from that 'royo, and we ought to foller his trail and see if we can figure out what happened. 'Course we don't know if he rode straight there or if he rode down some more 'royos tryin' to lose 'em."

"He couldn't lose them that way, could he?"

"Not for long. Maybe he hoped they would ride past 'im and he could double back to town or to the ranch."

"Obviously, it didn't work. And it's going to be hard to track him after all the rain. Do you suppose he threw those saddlebags into one of those ravines?"

"That's about all we've got to hope for, ain't it? And hope we can find 'em."

She was thoughtful. "Yes, that's what we're here for, and I'm afraid our chances aren't too good. I mean, if his killers couldn't find them, how are we going to?"

"Listen, you and your uncle know—knew—this country. Can you think of any likely hidin' place?"

"I've been thinking, and the answer is no. This country is full of washes and arroyos. If those saddlebags are in one of them, it will take some good old-fashioned luck to find them."

J.B. leaned back on his elbows, feet to the fire. The night outside the circle of firelight was black, except for the stars overhead. The soft voice of a ground owl came to them. The fire crackled.

"All we can do," he thought aloud' "is try like a steer." Then he realized what he had said. "Excuse me, Miss Crandall. I didn't mean to, uh—I'm not used to campin' with girls."

"Call me Shine." That was all she had to say on that subject. She pulled her boots off and crawled inside the sleeping bag and, sitting up, started fastening the buttons. When she had the bag buttoned halfway up, she lay back and pulled the edge over her.

J.B. pulled off his boots, carefully placed them in the bottom end of the folded bed tarp, placed the .45 beside him, and lay back between the folds with his hands under his head. "Anyway," he said, "it don't look like rain tonight."

She didn't answer. He looked over at her and saw she was asleep. He lay awake awhile, listening to the muffled popping of the dying fire, listened to the munching and snorting of the grazing horses, thought about how pleasant it was to be looking up at the stars instead of the ceiling of a jail, wondered how this episode in his life was going to turn out, then finally dozed off himself.

CHAPTER 12

Cowboys, accustomed to rolling out at first light, can't sleep well after dawn, and J.B. was up and building a fire when she awakened. She yawned, stretched, and started unbuttoning the sleeping bag. "Good morning," she said cheerfully. "Brrr, it's cold before sunup."

"Mornin'." He grinned and nodded at the sleeping bag. "Sometime somebody's gonna git buttoned up in one of them and won't be able to git out."

"It's not the best bed in the world, but it's easy to carry behind a saddle." She crawled out of the sleeping bag, sat on it, and pulled on her boots. "Breakfast without coffee will be strange, but the steaks will taste good and they'll stick to our ribs."

She stood up and warmed herself by the fire, then went to the creek and washed her face in cold water. "Brrr. Boy, that will sure get the sleep out of your eyes."

"It'll start you quick and run you slick," J.B. grinned.

Again, they warmed the meat and biscuits by holding them over the fire on green sticks. They ate, put out the fire, and went for the horses.

Once mounted, they laid out a plan of action. "Do you think we need to go back to where you found the slicker?" she asked.

"No, that's been pretty well searched. Can you point in the direction where the dead horse is?"

She pointed north by northeast. "It has to be in that direction."

"Then let's see if we can cut their sign." He rode away to the east, in a direction that would cross any trail the pursued and the pursuers left. She followed.

"Are you a good tracker, J.B.?"

"Not the best, but I've picked up a few ol' cows I would've missed if I'd been a plum greenhorn." He rode silently a mile, eyes to the ground, then stopped. "Here it is."

She looked at where he was pointing and looked at him. "I don't see anything."

He grinned. "That's the kind of readin' you don't learn at no university." He dismounted and pointed with his finger at an almost invisible indentation in the ground and at a small rock that was out of place and on its edge. "They was foggin' it, too," he said, pointing to a yucca that was misshapen. "A horse won't run over one of them 'less somebody's makin' spur tracks on 'im."

"Oh. Can you tell how many horses were in the race?"

Without answering, he mounted and rode away, still studying the ground. Soon he stopped again. "There was three horses in the race, and here's the sign of two more. They was all rained on, but them tracks"—he pointed to the right of where his horse was standing— "was made a day or so later, and they're headin' into that draw over there."

"Then we guessed right," she said. "We aren't the only ones looking for that money. They searched the draws after Uncle Len was killed."

"Yep. It's the same two that chased 'im, and they had the same idea we had."

"Are you sure there are only two?"

"Yep. One of 'em changed horses, but the other'n is ridin' the same horse he rode when they took after your uncle."

"Dutch Schultz and who?"

"Aw, come on, Shine, you know who." He was grinning a crooked grin.

"I think I do, but I want to hear you say it. To see if you're thinking the same thing I am."

"All right, I'll say it: John Buetel."

"You're not just saying that because of the way he treated you?"

"Nope."

"Why do you suspect him?"

"Several reasons. Why do you suspect 'im?"

She was pensive. "First, he is the only one who knew Uncle Len would be going to town with his saddlebags full of money. And second, because he would profit two ways: he would get the money, half of it anyway, and he would get the CC Ranch."

"You're brilliant," J.B. chided, copying a word from her "And I can add a couple more."

"Speak, cowboy."

"He wanted me hung. It was his idea, according to Ol' Derby Hat. I overheard 'im say ol' Buetel was disappointed when I got away. He wanted me hung because he figured that *pendejo* sheriff would sooner or later find the body, and would consider the mystery solved and the killer gone to his just rewards."

"He was probably right, too," she said. "What else?"

"Ol' Derby Hat, or Schultz, or whatever his name was, was shot in the back."

"By John Buetel," she said. "Because," she added thoughtfully, "after what Dutch Schultz did to us he was in trouble with the law, and his *compadre* in my uncle's murder didn't want him arrested and interrogated, and maybe spilling the beans."

J.B. added, "That makes it look like his *compadre* is somebody that belongs here and cain't just ride on."

"And that spells John Buetel," she said with finality.

J.B. held the bridle reins between two fingers of his left hand and rolled a smoke. He bent his head down so he could lick the paper without moving his rein hand. "But all that don't solve your problem, Shine."

"Correct, cowboy. We can't prove a thing, and we still don't have that money."

They rode on, in and out of the draws and ravines, eyes constantly searching. The sun climbed higher. Miss Crandall often shifted her weight in the saddle. The cowboy noticed, but said nothing. At one point, J.B. lost the tracks and had to go back a quarter mile to pick them up again. He apologized. "I was lookin' too far ahead."

"No apology is necessary, J.B. If it weren't for your rangeland skills, we would be facing a hopeless puzzle."

"Don't be pattin' me on the back yet. The puzzle is still a puzzle."

"I have a feeling, J.B., that if we continue following these tracks we'll learn something."

Reining up suddenly, J.B. allowed, "Well, I already learned somethin', but I don't know if it makes any difference."

"What, J.B."

"They gave up the hunt right here. They stopped and palavered some, then rode off toward town. Must've been gettin' dark on 'em."

"Wonderful. That means they didn't find anything."

J.B. touched spurs to the blue-roan and rode on, leaning forward and low in his saddle, looking at the ground, looking ahead. He stopped again. "But they came back. Prob'ly the next day."

"Oh. Well, I guess we couldn't expect them to have given up."

"They wasn't about to."

On they went. The girl rode up beside him and asked, "How can you tell so much from tracks? I mean, how do you know which horses were chasing which?"

He answered without taking his eyes off the ground. "It's easy. Your uncle was riding a good-sized horse, prob'ly around twelve hundred pounds, and that was the horse that was bein' chased."

"How can you tell?"

"By the size of his feet. He took a Number One shoe. He left a good track way back there, and I could see he was bigger than the other two horses."

"You're right. Red Feather is bigger than most horses. Rather, he was. But how could you tell which horses were chasing which?"

He glanced at her, then looked down again. "Back there—I don't see any good tracks here—but back there one of the other horses stepped on a track left by the big horse. That means the big horse had to of been in front."

"Of course. And you know by the size of the hoofprints that one of the pursuers changed horses before they came back."

"It was easier than that. The fresh horse had feet kind of like a mule. You know, not quite as round in the forefeet."

"Of course."

It was close to noon when they found the saddlebags.

The bags were on the ground at the bottom of the deep grassy draw, and were easy to see. When J.B. spotted them, he booted the blue-roan into a gallop and dismounted on the run. The girl was on the ground three seconds behind him, happy at their find. "It's them. It's Uncle Len's saddlebags."

Together they grabbed them up and put their hands inside, searching for money. They were empty.

J.B. dropped the bags onto the ground and made a sour face. "Well, they got it."

Disappointment brought a long sigh of hopelessness from her. Her shoulders slumped. "Looks like it. It had to have been the men who killed Uncle Len."

"They're just luckier than us, I guess," the cowboy said.

"Luck," she said bitterly. "Why do the wicked have all the luck?" She sat dejectedly on a large rock, hanging onto the ends of her bridle reins. "Do you mind if I swear, J.B.?"

He shrugged. "There's a few words I'd rather not hear a lady say, but other than them, go ahead."

She cut loose in Spanish with a long sentence that included at least two *chingaos*, a *pendejo*, and a *cabrón*. J.B. chuckled. She frowned and continued in Spanish until she was out of breath. Then she was silent.

She sat on her rock and the cowboy squatted on his heels, and they stared at the ground. Finally she asked, "What are you thinking?"

He took his time answering. "We have to find a way to prove he did it." He paused for a long moment, then: "And I just cain't think of one."

"Neither can I," she said gloomily.

He banged his fist against his knee. "There's got to be a way. We cain't let 'im get by with it. Think."

"I'm thinking."

J.B. stood up and began walking, head down. He uttered several emphatic "Damns." She also stood up and began walking. A few more *chingaos* and *pendejos* came out of her.

Suddenly she stopped and stood still. "J.B." Her voice was

excited. "J.B., come here."

He limped to her. "There," she said, pointing at the ground. "It's a sandwich wrapper. Wax paper. The kind we have at the house. And there," she pointed to a scrap of bread nearby. "It's the remains of Uncle Len's lunch. He had his lunch in those saddlebags."

J.B. agreed. "It's what's left after the satchel birds and pocket gophers got through with it."

"Do you know what this might mean, J.B.?" She was looking into his eyes, her voice excited.

"What it might mean? It means he carried a sandwich in his saddlebags. So what?"

"It might mean—I'm not sure—but it might mean his lunch was *all* he carried in those bags."

Pushing his hat back and wiping sweat from his forehead, J.B. tried to read her thoughts. "Are you tryin' to tell me he might not've had that money with him after all?"

"It's possible. Think about it."

"I'm thinkin'."

She slapped her thigh and clapped her hands with exuberance. "It could be the answer." Her voice rose. "It could be the reason he threw away his slicker and the gold coins."

J.B. squinted at her, his mind working, trying to see what she was getting at. It began to come to him. "Let me ask you one question, Shine: did your uncle always carry saddlebags?"

"He always did. And you know as well as I do, J.B., that cowboys seldom carry anything on their saddles except a rope and maybe a slicker in rainy season."

"Uh huh," he exclaimed. "So when he threw away his slicker they didn't even notice it 'cause all they could think about was what they thought was in those saddlebags."

"Exactly. They didn't know he always carried them, and assumed that they were full of money. After all, he said he was going to be carrying money. He let them chase him several miles from the gold coins, and when he was out of sight briefly in this draw, he hid the saddlebags. He hoped that when they noticed he no longer had them, they would quit chasing him and go back and look for the money."

"And," J.B. took up the premise, "he knew they wouldn't git any of his money 'cause he'd dropped all he had with him way back there end there wasn't any money in these." He nodded toward the saddlebags. "But he was wrong about one thing."

"They continued chasing him. Do you suppose he didn't recognize John Buetel?"

"Could be he didn't. He didn't know, I guess, he was bein' chased by a so-called prominent citizen that couldn't let him live to talk about it." J.B. pronounced the words "prominent citizen" as if they tasted bad.

Her exuberance faded and her voice took on a sad note. "They had to kill him, didn't they? But first they had to torture him and try to make him tell where he had hidden the money."

"Yeah. Looks like they didn't find them 'til later." He pointed to the saddlebags. "But," he turned to the girl, his eyes puzzled, "why in the humped-up world did he tell ol' Buetel he was comin' to town with a load of money?"

"Because he was ornery as well as eccentric. He and John Buetel hated each other. He had the banker all primed to receive a lot of money that could be invested in more land, and I'm guessing he planned to pay just enough to forestall foreclosure and make him wait for the rest. He would have enjoyed seeing the disappointment on Buetel's face."

"He was ornery enough to do a thing like that?"

"He was the most cantankerous man I've ever known."

"If that's what happened, his orneriness got him killed. It was a fool thing to do."

"Oh," she said, her voice calm now, "he didn't trust John Buetel and he hated him, but he didn't suspect he could commit murder."

"Some of the worst crooks I ever heard of was prominent citizens."

"Yes. For enough money—and hatred—I suppose even a banker can commit murder."

"Well," J.B. said, scratching his jaw, "that could explain it. He didn't intend to pay off the whole note after all."

"It makes sense, doesn't it?"

"Yep. Judgin' from what you told me about your uncle, I can

believe it."

"And in the meantime, he made Buetel pay through the nose for the hay he had to have to feed those beeves in the railroad pens."

"Which didn't make the banker exactly fall in love with 'im."

J.B. chuckled. "It ain't funny, what happened to your uncle, but ol' Buetel must've had a conniption fit when he finally found them saddlebags and opened 'em up."

"All he got was a sandwich," she said.

The cowboy was walking around with his head down, studying the ground again. He looked over at Miss Crandall and shrugged. "It's all here. Just the way you figured it. I should've seen it before, but I guess I was too happy at findin' the saddlebags."

"Seen what, J.B.?"

"The sign. Look," he pointed at the ground. "Len Crandall stopped here for a minute and hid them saddlebags behind that rock, the one you was settin' on, then got back on his horse and went on. The two *hombres* chasin' 'im didn't see 'im stop, and they kept right after 'im. It was later that ol' Buetel and his sidekick backtracked and found 'em."

"Poor Uncle Len." Her voice was strained. "He tried, J.B." She was silent a moment, then she groaned, "Oh my God."

It was his turn to ask, "What?"

Tears had come to her eyes. "It just occurred to me. His horse was shot down and they were probably mean enough to make him walk up that canyon trail with a rope around his neck, dragging him when he couldn't keep up. Oh my God."

J.B.'s jaw was tight as he absorbed what she had said. "I try not to cuss around women, Shine, but there's some folks you cain't talk about without cussin'. Them two're pure, genuine, all-wool sonsofbitches."

"And still, he wouldn't tell them anything."

"He must've been some feller, that uncle of your's."

"He was. He was eccentric, ornery, cantankerous. But he never mistreated anyone who didn't deserve it. And he was my uncle."

"Yeah. He didn't take off for the big city with the ranch's money after all."

"I'm so sorry," She put her face in her hands. "How could I

139

have thought such a thing."

He tried to think of something to say to make her feel better, but words failed him. She sniffed her nose and wiped it with a dainty handkerchief. "I was wrong. They tortured him and he wouldn't tell."

"Looks like it. But I can understand why you would think what you thought. Anybody might've. Don't blame yourself, Shine. You didn't ask 'im to do what he done and git hisself killed."

J.B. had said all he could say, done all he could do. He walked slowly back to the horses and picked up his bridle reins. He waited until she had had her cry, and when she was through, she joined him.

"Well, anyhow," he said, "we solved the mystery. But we still lost the money."

"Why?" She looked at him, eyes still moist.

"'Cause if your uncle didn't have it with him, it's in the main house, and if ol' Buetel's livin' in that house now, he's bound to've found it."

"No, I don't think so."

"No?"

"Uncle Len liked to hoard money, and he had an ingenious hiding place."

"You don't think they found it, even with all the time and privacy in the world?"

"It's possible, but I don't think so."

"You know where his hidin' place is?"

"Yes."

"Then we have to git it."

Her eyes brightened. "Yes."

CHAPTER 13

The more they thought about it, the more excited they became. It would be dangerous, they knew, and there was a good chance it would be all for nothing. But they had to try.

They ate the last of the beef and biscuits and decided to pass up supper rather than go to town and come back again. By the time they had cleaned up the last crumb, it was definite. They had to wait until after dark, but they would raid the CC ranch house that night.

They mounted again and rode to a grassy hillside four miles from the house, off-saddled the horses, and let them graze while they made plans.

"Yes. When my dad and Uncle Len built the house they wanted the most modern conveniences money could buy," she said. "That included running water. So they built in a five-hundred-gallon water tank right inside the house, between the walls."

They were sitting cross-legged facing each other while she told about it. "Every drop of snow and rain water that falls on the roof ends up in that tank, and during the dry seasons, water from Juniper Creek can be diverted to it also.

"The result is, when anyone turns on a faucet on the ground floor of the house, gravity forces the water to gush through it. We even have a fifty-gallon tank on the back porch with a wood-burning firebox built under it. We actually have hot and cold running water."

J.B. had picked up a small stick and was drawing lines on the ground with it. "I've heard of a ranch house with runnin' water, I don't think I've ever seen one. Most business buildings in most towns have runnin' water nowadays. Anyhow," he looked up, "what's all this got to do with the CC Ranch money?"

"That's Uncle Len's hiding place. He had his hoard wrapped in heavy oilskin sitting on the bottom of that tank. It's on the southeast corner. You have to fish it out from the second-floor opening. Uncle Len has it double wrapped and he has a heavy wire bale on it, sticking straight up. He had a long piece of heavy wire with a hook on the end of it and he used that to hook the bale and bring up his hoard.

"Now," she leaned back, a smug expression on her face, "do you think John Buetel and his hoodlums will find it?"

J.B. shook his head and grinned. "Your Uncle must of been some *hombre*. But," he asked, "didn't you look, after your uncle disappeared, to see if he had any money there?"

"No. I should have. But he said he was taking it all to pay off the bank, and I thought that was what he did."

J.B. shook his head again. "He must of been some *hombre loco*."

Her head came up and she snapped, "Okay, I said he was eccentric. He was very eccentric. But he was my uncle and he showed me his hiding place. He wasn't hiding money from me."

"It's no skin off my nose," J.B. said. "Now we've got to find a way to look at that hidey-stash." He pondered the problem a moment, then, "You say he had a wire hook he fished it out with? Where did he keep that hook?"

"On the back porch. Oh, I see what you're getting at. No, he didn't leave it near the tank opening as a dead giveaway that something besides water was inside

"If ol' Buetel seen it on the back porch, he prob'ly wouldn't guess in a hundred years what it was for, huh?"

"That's something we have to assume."

J.B. resumed scratching on the ground. He squinted at the sky. "Won't be dark for four or five hours. Wonder when ol' Buetel goes to bed?"

"I don't know. What we have to do is tie the horses in the scrub cedars south of the house and sneak up on foot. I'm just hoping he didn't bring a strange dog to the ranch. I know Old Tip. He's been everyones pet for years, and he won't bark at me."

"Wonder how many men're sleepin' in that house?"

"I don't know. It's chancy, J.B. We could be shot. You don't have to go with me if you don't want to. In fact, maybe it would be easier for me to do it alone. Four feet would make more noise."

His head came up then. "You gettin' eccentric too? Listen, that's not my money, but I owe ol' Buetel. He's the cause of all my troubles. I owe that son of a..."

"*Puta*," she finished the statement for him.

"Correct," he said, again using one of her words.

"Anyhow." He lay back on the grass, put his hat over his face and his hands under his head. "I'm goin' in there with you." He lifted his hat, glanced over at her, and added, "That's final."

She picked up a pebble and tossed it at him, that beginning of a smile on her face again. It fell on his chest. "Assertive, aren't you," she said. He picked up the pebble and tossed it back at her. She punched him playfully on the shoulder. He punched her on the shoulder. She punched him harder with a small, feminine fist. He grabbed her wrist. She pulled back and struggled, giggling. He let go. She punched him again and he grabbed her wrist again. She punched him with the other fist and he grabbed that wrist.

They rolled on the ground, laughing. "J.B.," she shrieked. "Stop it, J.B." He relaxed his hold and she rolled on top of him. He pushed her off and rolled over so the upper half of his body covered her from the waist up.

He was looking down at her, into her blue eyes. Her body was soft and feminine. Her blond hair was in her face. Her teeth were white and perfect as she smiled up at him. The young cowboy felt a terrible urgency well up inside him. The smile left his face.

She knew what was happening, and she too stopped smiling. "No, J.B. Not now. Not here."

He was drawn to her, to those soft lips, those pearly teeth. She pushed at him. "J.B., stop it." She pushed harder. He threw himself off and rolled onto his back, breathing in short, shallow gasps. He picked up the pistol that had fallen onto the ground and shoved it back inside his belt. She sat up and brushed the hair from her eyes.

"I'm sorry. I started that. I shouldn't have."

He grabbed his hat and slammed it over his face again. "Yeah," he said, his voice muffled by the hat.

At dusk they saddled up. They spoke little as they rode toward the ranch. Each wondered privately what the night would bring, whether they would find the money and whether they would get away if they did. By the time they reached the first fence, it was dark and J.B. had to rely on the girl to lead the way. There was no moon and no light.

They followed the fence until they came to the road leading from the ranch to El Rey and they turned up the road. A mile farther on, she stopped. He could see a dense growth of some kind to the south of the road, and guessed it was the buck brush, what she had called scrub cedars.

"Try to pick out a landmark, will you," she said. "We'd better leave the horses here and go on foot the rest of the way."

He looked around carefully, and all he could see in the dark was a subtle change in darkness where the thicket joined the vega. "I think I can find it," he said.

They dismounted and groped for scrub cedar limbs to tie their horses to. J.B. hefted the pistol once to assure himself he still had it, and placed it back inside his belt. "The buildings are just around the curve in the road," she said.

They walked silently around the curve, and the lights from the main house and the bunkhouse came into view. J.B. was still limping, but he had no trouble keeping up. As they got closer, they could see the outline of the main house, as well as lights flickering on both Boors.

"I think," the girl said, "that this is as far as we should go now. Let's sit down here and wait until the lights go out."

They sat cross-legged in the high center of the road, between two wagon ruts. Once they saw a shadow pass a first-floor window in the house, and then they saw another in a second-floor window. "There's at least two people in that house," J.B. remarked.

"John Buetel is a bachelor," the girl said, "but he could have one or more of his henchmen living in the house with him, or perhaps one or more members of the bank board as guests."

"The tank has to be on the north side of the house if it gets

144

water from the creek," J.B. guessed, "and his bedroom's on the south side. That's in our favor."

"Yes, my bedroom was on the north side, across the hall from the tank opening. I hope no one is sleeping in it."

They waited in silence for a time. Then the girl said, "This is terribly dangerous, J.B. I can't let you risk your life this way for nothing. If the money is there and we succeed, half of it is yours."

"Oh, no. No, ma'am. That's your money. You don't owe me nothin'."

"We'll see about that."

He was about to ask what she meant when the light on the first floor went out. Her breath caught momentarily in her throat, and J.B.'s breathing became shallow in anticipation of what was soon to happen. Next, the dim light in the bunkhouse went out, and a few minutes later the main house was dark.

"We'd better give them another half hour to doze off," she whispered.

"Maybe we can git a little closer." He found himself whispering too, even though they were a good distance from the house. "That dog is goin' to bark at us, and I'd rather git that over now."

"Good thinking. It's better to have Old Tip bark now than later after they fall asleep."

They stood up and walked quietly toward the house. The dog heard them coming and let out two "Whoofs."

"It's Old Tip," she said. "That's good. They won't pay any attention to that. He's always barking at coyotes or something."

The dog let out two more "Whoofs," this time closer.

"He's coming to investigate," she whispered. Then, in a louder whisper, "Here, Tip. Here, boy."

They heard the dog panting, heard its footsteps, then its nose was in Miss Crandall's face, and it was jumping with the joy of seeing its master again.

"Down boy," she whispered. "It's good to see you too, old fella. Stay down now."

The dog sniffed once at J.B., immediately lost interest in him, and concentrated on trying to lick the girl's face. She rubbed and scratched the animal. "Down, boy. Good boy."

Another twenty minutes passed before they decided to go on with their mission. The dog stayed beside them as they walked slowly, carefully, into the yard. "We'll go in the back door," she whispered, "and get the hook, then we'll have to climb the stairs. It will be black as pitch in there, but I know every inch of the house. You follow me. Put your hand on my shoulder and walk behind me."

The darkness changed to blackness ahead of them as they approached the house. They were now walking on a strip of flat stones that had been set flush with the ground to form a path. Then the back porch was ahead of them. The first obstacle was the screen door. It was fastened. "It's just a wirehook," she whispered. "Use your pocket-knife blade to slip between the door and the frame and push up." He did so, and felt the hook lift out of the eye of the latch.

She turned the knob on the porch door slowly, ever so carefully. A slight click, and the door cracked open. She pushed it halfway open and the dark interior of the house loomed before them. Without stepping through the door, she reached inside, around the door frame.

"It should be right here," she whispered, barely audibly. "Ah, here it is." She put her mouth close to J.B.'s ear. "Okay, I've got the hook. The back door is probably open. Here we go."

J.B. grabbed the butt of the six-gun and held it in his right hand while he put his left hand on her shoulder. She moved stealthily and stopped when she came to the door that separated the kitchen from the porch. "Step up," she whispered.

He felt her shoulder lift, and he moved his feet carefully, feeling for the door jamb. He found it, stepped over, and they were in the kitchen. Afraid to communicate at all now, they slid their feet softly over the linoleum floor. When she made a sharp right turn, he guessed she was going around a kitchen table, and he hoped there were no chairs in their path. He blinked his eyes repeatedly, trying to become accustomed to the darkness. It was useless. The interior of the house was black.

She stopped again, and they stood for a long moment, breathing shallowly. All was quiet. When she moved again, he followed, and found himself on a carpet. Again she stopped, felt for his face with one hand, and put her mouth next to his left ear. Her breath tickled.

"The stairs are just ahead. Keep your feet on the edges, and maybe they won't creak." Her voice was so low he had to think about her words before he understood what she had said.

Taking steps of only a few inches' at a time, they made their way across a wide room. The carpet muffled all sound. J.B. tried to picture in his mind the layout. He knew they would have to turn left to approach the stairs. Slowly, she turned left. He followed. The stairs were carpeted, but the wooden structure groaned like a pained whisper under their weight. They stopped immediately and listened. The house was quiet. More low groans accompanied their progress, and a barely audible squeak came from a step as J.B.'s foot lifted from it. Again they stopped and listened.

CHAPTER 14

J.B. guessed they had to be near the top of the stairs now. He wanted to hear snores coming from the bedrooms, but he heard no sound at all.

Another squeak sounded, this one more audible, as she reached the top. He guessed from the sound that it was the next to last step that squeaked, and he took a long step, lifting his foot over it, to get to the top. He collided gently with her when he got to the top. They listened—and heard the snores.

She moved on and J.B. followed. He found himself next to a wall, placed the gun inside his belt, put his hand on the wall, and used it and her shoulder as a guide. The hallway was carpeted too, reminding J.B. that he was in the home of a well-to-do family. Or rather it used to be the home of a family. Now it was occupied by a thief and a murderer.

She turned to the left and stopped. Again she put her mouth to J.B.'s ear. "Here's the tank door. Feel of it." He stepped up beside her and groped the wall with his hands. He found a metal door about waist high and groped for the latch, then remembered that she knew exactly where it was. He stepped back, and she took over.

All J.B. could do then was stand there and try to breath quietly. He heard metal scrape metal as the latch was lifted. He heard metal hinges squeak dangerously loud, heard her intake of breath. He put his hand on her shoulder again and realized she was trembling. He wondered whether she would be able to go on with it, then felt her shoulder move again as she continued to push the door open, one careful inch at a time. She pushed the door. Hinges squeaked. She pushed it another inch. Hinges squeaked. They listened. The snoring continued. She pushed the door another inch and again the hinges squeaked.

She stood still, and they listened. The snoring stopped and bedsprings creaked. They almost stopped breathing. For a long moment they stood there. J.B. could still feel the girl trembling, and he wished he could do something for her. He wanted to hold her hands, talk to her. But that was impossible.

He gripped the pistol butt, half expecting a light to appear with a gun behind it. At least he would know where to shoot. Any light Buetel or his henchmen had would make a good target, while he and the girl would be in the dark. But they were in a narrow hallway and would be hard to miss if enough bullets were scattered around. He decided that if shooting started, he would grab the girl and throw her and himself to the floor.

Then suddenly the snoring resumed.

He felt, rather than heard, the girl exhale, felt her moving again, felt the end of the long wire she carried touch his face like a cold finger as she put the hook end through the tank door.

With his hand on her shoulder, he heard a faint splash as the wire went into the water, felt her bend over and put her head and shoulders through the door. She was still trembling. He heard the hook thud gently against the side of the tank and heard her intake of breath.

She paused, and again they listened. The snoring had changed pitch but was still audible. Her shoulder moved again. Then she whispered, "I think I've got it." A pause. "Yes, I've got it. Help me."

He reached inside the tank and took hold of the wire. Yes, there was something on the end of it. He pulled it up hand over hand. Water splashed as something bulky cleared the water line. Excited now, he pulled it up and got his hands on it. It was slick oilskin. He got hold of the wire bale and lifted. He had his hands on a bundle wrapped in thick oilskin, exactly the way she had described it. He was holding a fortune.

They were both breathing audibly with the excitement as he

pulled the bundle through the tank door. "Careful," she whispered.

He tried, but the bundle was heavy and he couldn't see the edges of the door. The bundle banged against an edge with a loud thud.

They stood stock still. The snoring ended with a loud snort, bedsprings squealed, and feet hit the floor.

"That you, Obie? Somebody's out there. Who's out there?"

J.B. recognized the voice of John Buetel, and knew from what was said that another man was in one of the other upstairs bedrooms.

A match was scratched and a lamp was lit. The bedroom door was open. There was no use tiptoeing now, J.B. knew. They had to run. The girl had the same thought.

She grabbed J.B. by the arm. "This way," she said.

He hefted the bundle under his left arm, gripped the six-gun in his right hand, and let her lead him to the stairs. She ran down the steps, pulling him along, and once he missed a step and fell heavily against the banister. He kept his feet, however, and took a new hold on the bundle as he took the steps as rapidly as he could.

Shouts came from behind them. A shot was fired. The bullet hit the bundle J.B. was carrying and almost knocked it out of his grasp. He tightened his hold on it and willed his feet to move faster.

Then they were down the stairs and the girl pulled him straight ahead toward the front door. "No," he said. "Not that way."

She understood immediately and turned to the kitchen, pulling them around a corner where bullets fired from the head of the stairs couldn't reach them.

He ran over a kitchen chair and dropped his bundle. He picked it up and threw it on his shoulder and followed her in the darkness. They were through the kitchen and on the back porch when the next shots came.

A kitchen pot clanked as a bullet hit it. Another bullet splintered the floor inches from J.B.'s left foot.

The girl yanked open the screen door and they were outside. A figure was running toward them from the bunkhouse, yelling, "What is it? What's goin' on?" The dog was barking at the excitement.

"Run," J.B. said.

"I'm running."

The weight of the bundle caused him to stagger and his left foot was still sore, but he gritted his teeth and ran. They made it out of the yard and onto the road before more shooting came from behind them. J.B. thanked his lucky stars for the darkness. No bullets came close.

She was two steps ahead of him when he fell. It was the high center of the road that he stubbed his left foot on, and he took a nose dive, dropping the bundle and the gun. A loud "Ooh" came out of him. She was at his side, trying to pull him to his feet. "I dropped it," he hissed. His groping hands soon found the oilskin bundle, but he couldn't find the gun.

She knelt and searched the ground with her hands, then whispered, "I found the gun, did you find the money?"

"Yeah, let's go."

He was happy to let her carry the gun as he used both hands to hold the bundle on his right shoulder. He ran a ways, then shifted it to his left shoulder again. She was still ahead of him.

Someone behind them shouted, "They're on the road. They got to be on the road. Shoot down the road."

Another voice yelled, "Git some horses."

Gunfire came fast and furious, and bullets kicked up dirt around them and whistled a deadly song over their heads.

"Damn," he said through clenched teeth. "Git off the road."

She grabbed his arm and led him off the road past a small clump of scrub cedar. "We can cut across here," she gasped. "Here's a shallow draw. Watch your step."

His feet dropped into the draw, but he kept his balance and kept running, hoping he wouldn't stub his toe again.

"Here's the road," she said, breathing hard. They were back on the road, around the bend, out of sight of the house. But their pursuers were still coming. Booted feet pounded the road.

"We've got to stop 'em," J.B. panted. "Gimme that gun."

"I'll do it. You hang onto that money."

"Can you shoot?"

"I can shoot."

She ran back around the curve to where she could see dim figures running toward them. She took the pistol in both hands and cocked the hammer back. Squinting her eyes closed, she held the pistol at arm's length, turning her head away at the same time. The gun was unsteady but pointed in the right direction as she pulled the trigger.

The big six-shooter bucked in her hands, causing her to stagger back two steps, and the explosion almost deafened her. Still holding it as far away from her as she could, she cocked the hammer back and fired again. Then again.

"Give 'em another," J.B. yelled.

The six-gun boomed and bucked again. A man yelped. The footsteps ceased.

"Let's run," he shouted.

"I'm running."

The horses snorted at the running humans and the gunshots. They stamped their feet and danced around on the end of their bridle reins. That made it easy for J.B. and the girl to find them. Even the normally steady blue-roan was nervous when J.B. threw the bundle across the front of the saddle and groped for the stirrup. He found the stirrup and mounted, feeling awkward with the bundle in the saddle with him. He held onto it with one hand and spun the horse around to the road with the other.

"Are you horseback?" he asked, not bothering to whisper.

"I'm horseback."

"Let's ride."

"I'm riding."

Again the cow pony jumped out in the lead, but again the longer-legged blue-roan caught up and could have gone on by. But this time, J.B. held it back and kept pace with the girl. He was sitting high on the cantle to make room for the package on the saddle in front of him. He was uncomfortable.

"It's another horse race," the girl shouted.

"Yeah, but I think we've got a good head start."

"I hope I'm not mistaken about what's in that bundle."

"It feels like a bunch of straw, but we won't know for sure 'till we open 'er up."

"Hang onto it."

"I'm hangin' onto it."

They rode side by side on the wagon road, their horses running full gallop. The girl leaned forward to duck the wind but J.B., riding cowboy style, sat straight up and let the wind whistle around his ears. He tipped his head a little to let the wind push his hat down tighter, instead of blowing it off.

"I hate to ask a dumb question," he yelled at the girl, "but where're we goin'?"

"El Rey. The sheriff's office. It's the only safe place."

"Is there anybody there at night?"

"The sheriff sleeps in the back room. We'll roust him out."

"We'd better slow down and pace these ol' ponies."

"You're right. They can't run all the way to town."

She hauled the cowpony down to a slow gallop, and J.B. slowed the blue-roan also.

"Do you know where we are?" he asked.

"We've got another four or five miles to go. Wonder if there's anyone behind us."

"If there ain't, there will be. Listen for 'em. We cain't let 'em git too close."

"I'm listening."

They rode another mile at a slow gallop, then heard hoofbeats pounding the road behind them. "Goose that pony," J.B. shouted.

The horses, already winded, were prodded to run faster. They ran faster. A shot came from behind them. Another. J.B. knew the men were shooting down the road in hopes of blindly hitting a horse and ending the chase. He figured they had a fair chance of success. He tried to figure a way to defend himself and the girl if one of their horses was hit.

"Have you still got the gun?" he shouted.

"I've still got it."

"Hang onto it. I'd take it but my hands are full."

"I'm hanging onto it."

If a horse was shot down, J.B. decided, they would try to reach El Rey on foot in the dark. He would send the other horse on down the road in hopes the men would follow it. He could only hope that neither he nor the girl would be injured if a horse fell.

Gunfire came furiously, but the road was full of gentle curves and no bullets came close. J.B. felt the blue-roan tiring and knew the other horse was tiring too.

"Not much farther," the girl shouted.

They topped a hill and saw a dim light ahead, and J.B. knew they would soon be riding downhill onto El Rey's main street. He tightened his grip on the bundle and took a long look behind him. He saw a vague shape moving in the darkness and estimated it was six hundred yards away.

Then they were riding at a dead run down the main street, their horses hooves beating a tattoo on the packed dirt. They headed for the lighted window in the sheriff's office. "Let's cut around and go down the alley," she yelled. "We can knock on the back door."

"There's a light in the front winder," J.B. yelled. "Maybe somebody's up."

"No. They always leave a lamp lit."

The horses had run so far they were near the point of collapse, making it difficult to stop or turn them. Miss Crandall had to haul back on one rein to get her horse turned into the alley. The blue-roan turned with less difficulty. Then they were at the back of the sheriff's office, and the girl didn't try to stop her horse, just stepped off and let the animal go on. J.B. brought the blue-roan to a sliding stop, dropped his bundle on the ground, and stepped down. The horse trotted away, following the other horse.

She was at the back door, kicking at it, yelling, "Sheriff. Sheriff White. It's Shine Crandall. Sheriff!"

J.B. picked up the bundle, tucked it under his left arm, and took the pistol from the girl's hand. Hooves were thudding up the alley, and J.B. snapped a shot in that direction.

"Sheriff," the girl yelled. "It's Shine Crandall."

A horseman came up on a badly winded horse, and when he saw J.B.'s gun aimed at him he dropped off the horse and disappeared in the dark. More horsemen were coming, and J.B. fired again. They stopped. J.B. picked out the leader, aimed, and squeezed the trigger. The gun clicked harmlessly.

The horsemen heard the hammer strike an empty shell, and someone yelled, "Get them."

"Sheriff," the girl yelled.

Then the door swung open and Sheriff White was grumbling,

"What in thunderation's goin' on here," and the girl and J.B. ducked inside and slammed the door behind them.

Hoofbeats went past the door, but no more shots were fired. The room was in total darkness until Sheriff White scratched a match and held it up.

"Why, it is you, Miss Crandall. What in thunderation's goin' on? A feller'd think the 'Paches was comin'."

Feeling safe now, Miss Crandall let out a sigh. "It's a long story, sheriff, but we know who murdered Uncle Len, and we've got the money."

The sheriff stood there with his mouth open until the match burned down to his fingers. He dropped it suddenly and groped for another match. This time he lit a lamp. When he recognized J.B., his bushy eyebrows arched.

"You again. Danged if you ain't more trouble'n a tornado. What in thunderation's goin' on?"

Sheriff White was dressed in nothing but long underwear and boots. He looked down at himself, glanced at the girl and immediately blew out the lamp.

"A feller's got a right to get dressed in privacy," he said. "You go on out in the office and I'll be right there."

She said, "Strike another match, will you, sheriff, so we can find our way."

Another match was scratched and the sheriff handed it to her. "Right through that door there," he said. She led the way to the door, opened it, and went through. J.B. followed. He carried the oilskin bundle under his left arm and the six-gun in his right hand.

Once they were through the door, the lamp in the front office showed the way past the jail and into the office. J.B. put his bundle and gun down on the sheriff's desk and turned the lamp up. They looked around the room, looked at each other, then he fished his pocket knife out of his pocket.

"Let's see what we've got here," he said, as he cut the rope binding.

He had to cut through three rope bindings and unroll two yards of heavy oilskin before he could open the package. When he did, he couldn't help exhaling with relief.

He could think of no reason anyone would hide a bundle so carefully unless it contained something valuable, but knowing his luck, he couldn't help fearing that fate had played a dirty trick on him and the girl. But when the bundle was unwrapped, a pile of paper money was exposed in the lamplight.

For a moment, no one spoke, then J.B. said, "You guessed right, Shine."

She picked up a few bills and let them drop through her fingers. "Thank heavens," she sighed.

High-heeled boots clumped into the room, and Sheriff White walked up to his desk, running his fingers through his sparse hair. "Now what was—" He stopped and stared at the money. He stared with his mouth open, then timidly reached out and touched the pile. He picked up a bill and looked at it carefully in the lamplight. "I never saw so much money in my life," he said, almost whispering.

"It's hers," J.B. said matter-of-factly.

They all stared reverently at the pile of money on the sheriff's desk, then Sheriff White remembered his duties. He crossed the room and lit another lamp on a shelf, providing more light. He sat in the wooden chair behind his desk and let his eyes rove over J.B. and the girl.

"You said," he spoke slowly, "you know who murdered Len Crandall. Start talkin'."

Miss Crandall dropped into a chair opposite the desk. J.B. remained standing. "It was John Buetel and the man they called Dutch," she began. "They—"

Her words broke off as the front door slammed open. All eyes went to the door. John Buetel stood there.

156

CHAPTER 15

The banker was wearing ranch clothes and had a six-gun in a holster on his right hip. His black eyes took everything in before he entered the room and closed the door behind him. J.B. thought he looked more than ever like one of that new breed of Hereford bulls— all neck and body, with short legs.

Suddenly the six-gun was in Buetel's right hand, pointed at the sheriff. "Stand up, sheriff," he commanded.

For a moment, the sheriff kept his seat, blinking in disbelief at what was happening. "Stand up or I'll shoot you right here." Sheriff White slowly stood up.

"Now," the banker commanded, "I want you to stand on the other side of your desk, and you"—he waved his gun at J.B. and the girl—"stand over by that wall."

Sheriff White squawked, "What do you think you're doin', John? You can't—"

"Shut up. I know exactly what I'm doing." He studied the room and the people in it. "On second thought, you stand over by that jail door, sheriff, and you, cowboy, stand over here by this door."

Sheriff White stood petrified, staring at the husky man and the gun in his hand.

"Get moving, God damn it."

Moving as if his feet were too heavy, Sheriff White slumped by the jail door.

The gun shifted toward J.B. "You heard me, runt. You too.

157

Move, or I'll drop you right there."

The banker's face was granite hard, and his eyes were unblinking. There was no doubt in J.B.'s mind that he meant what he said. J.B. moved slowly to the door.

Buetel stepped away from the front door and stood in front of the sheriff's desk. "You," he said to Miss Crandall, "get over there by the sheriff." She did as she was told, and he surveyed the room again.

Sheriff White and the girl were standing across the room by the door that led to the jail, and J.B. was standing by the front door. J.B. was a few steps from the sheriff's desk and the pile of money and the gun he had placed on the desk.

Buetel stood on the other side of the desk, where he could see everyone in the room. "Yeah, that ought to do it," he said.

"What are you goin' to do, John?" Sheriff White asked nervously. "You can't get away with anything in here."

"Oh, can't I?" The banker's face was smug. "This is the perfect solution. Everyone knows you and this saddle bum here have had some harsh words. Everyone knows this *Tejano* is capable of anything. If he shoots you and the girl and you manage to shoot him before you die, that will end everything."

"But why?" the sheriff asked.

The girl spoke, holding Buetel's gaze. "You don't know yet, do you, Sheriff White? You don't know that John Buetel and Dutch Schultz waylaid Uncle Len, intending to kill him and take his money. You don't know that the only money Uncle Len had with him was the small pouch that J.B. found."

She turned to the sheriff. "But they thought he had two saddlebags full of money, and they planned to kill him for it. When they didn't find it, they took him up to that line camp and tortured and killed him, then dumped his body in the creek up there. Rain swelled the creek enough that it washed the body down into Juniper Creek, where J.B. found it."

Miss Crandall glanced at J.B., then at the gun on the desk, then at Buetel. J.B. knew she was sending him a silent message. He soon figured out what she was saying, but he doubted it would work.

"We found the empty saddlebags," she went on, "and got to thinking that perhaps Uncle Len didn't take the money with him after all. We sneaked into the CC house tonight and found it and brought it here. They chased us."

The sheriff was worried. He ran his fingers through his sparse hair. "It's hard to believe Mr. Buetel would do a thing like that. Why, he's been a fine citizen."

Again, the girl glanced at J.B. and at the gun on the desk. J.B. nodded imperceptibly.

"He's greedy," she said, looking back at the sheriff. It was obvious to J.B. that she was stalling for time. "Like most powerful men, he wanted more power. If he got his hands on the CC Ranch he would control the water in Juniper Creek, which would give him control over a lot of territory."

"All right," the banker cut in. "Now you all know why I have to kill you." He pointed the pistol menacingly at J.B, then at the sheriff. "Only we in this room know what happened. Soon, only I will know."

"What are you goin' to do, John?" the sheriff asked in a wavering voice.

J.B. weighed his chances. If something or someone would divert Buetel's attention for a second, he might have a chance. He would have to move as fast as he had ever moved in his life. He planned his moves in his mind. If J.B. was lucky, he could do it.

"What do you think?" The banker sneered. "I'm going to kill you and make it look like this bum here did it. Only, you are going to get in one shot. I'll have to shoot you two first, then I'll take your gun, sheriff, and shoot the cowboy, then I'll leave this gun in the cowboy's hand." He lifted the barrel of his six-gun, aimed at the sheriff.

"No, don't," the sheriff squawked. "Let's talk about this. Don't shoot."

Buetel's finger tightened on the trigger. A voice in J.B.'s mind screamed, "Now."

He dove head first behind the desk, his right arm up. At the instant he hit the floor, his right arm swept the gun off the desk onto the floor beside him. The desk was between him and Buetel.

But it wouldn't stop a bullet.

Buetel wheeled and fired. His shot was a hasty one and it tore through the desk over where J.B. lay flat on the floor. J.B. got the gun in his hand and cocked the hammer back.

He would have to shoot fast and accurately. One shot was all he would get. He had to jump up and shoot.

Buetel's second shot came at the instant J.B. jumped up. But the squat man fired low, trying to hit J.B. on the floor. The bullet burrowed into the floor near the cowboy's left boot. J.B. pointed the gun point blank at the banker's chest and squeezed the trigger. The gun only clicked. It was then J.B. remembered that all the cartridges in the gun had been fired.

Buetel knew. His lips skinned back from his teeth in a cruel grin. He could take his time. The sheriff wasn't armed, and the girl wasn't armed, and the cowboy's gun was empty. He chuckled.

J.B. saw death coming.

But suddenly Buetel had a wildcat on his back. In one long jump, Miss Crandall landed on him. The impact spoiled the banker's aim and his next shot went wild. She wrapped her arms around his face and her legs around his waist.

"Get him, J.B."

The cowboy grabbed for the banker's gun and got his left hand on it. His hand prevented Buetel from cocking the gun again, but J.B. couldn't twist it away from him.

"Hit him, J.B."

J.B. hit him. He swung the barrel of his own gun up against the side of Buetel's head. The banker staggered and went down.

J.B. kept his hold on the banker's pistol, trying to twist it free. He got his knee on Buetel's gun arm, but the big man was bucking and twisting under the weight of the girl and the cowboy, and still hanging onto the gun.

"Set on 'im," J.B. yelled.

"I'm sitting on him."

Again the cowboy slammed his pistol against the side of Buetel's head, and the banker went limp.

The girl stepped back. Her eyes shot sparks at the sheriff, who was standing by. "Take him. Lock him up." Only then did Sheriff White move. He knelt, ran his hands over the banker. He found another pistol, a small derringer, inside the right boot. White grabbed the banker under the armpits and dragged him backwards toward the jail. J.B. thought about helping him, then decided, to hell with it.

White dragged the semiconscious banker through the connecting door out of sight of J.B. and the girl.

They stood a few feet apart, facing each other. His hair was in her face. He stood with a gun in each hand, in his soiled new Levi's, one boot larger than the other, his eyebrows and hair singed, a blister on his face. She said softly, "You can put the guns down now."

He reached behind him and placed the pistols on the desk.

Then she was in his arms. "We did it, J.B. We did it. We won."

He wrapped his arms around her. He buried his face in her hair and tried to say something, but emotion choked off his words.

"We did it, J.B. Oh, we did it."

She took his face in her hands and kissed him full on the mouth. It was the sweetest kiss the cowboy had ever experienced. She wrapped her arms around J.B.'s neck and kissed him again. He hugged her tightly.

She pulled free and stood looking at him. Her eyes were moist, but she was smiling. "We got the money, and we'll get the ranch back, too. I know Judge Wilson won't let them keep the CC after he hears what happened."

His voice finally worked. "I'm just awful happy about that, Miss Crandall."

"Shine," she corrected him.

"Shine. You took a lot of dangerous chances. You're the bravest girl I ever heard of."

"You're the bravest. You're the greatest." She kissed him again. "You're my man."

They broke away from each other as the sheriff came back into the room. Sheriff White walked like a man only half alive, and sat wearily at his desk. "I don't think I was cut out to be a lawman," he sighed. "In the next election I'm goin' to run for county commissioner. That's an easier job. I'll be glad when this term is over."

He reached into a desk drawer and pulled out a writing tablet and a pencil. "I've got to get all this down in writin'. You two set down there and tell me everything that happened. Only, go slow, will you?"

Some of the paper money had been knocked off the desk onto

the floor during the struggle, and J.B. carefully gathered it up and rewrapped it all in the oilskin. The lawman flexed his fingers in anticipation of writer's cramps. "Let's hear it."

Shortly after daylight, Sheriff White's slow-talking, lanky deputy came in, listened awhile, and went back to the jail to see for himself that John Buetel was locked up. "He's alive and settin' up," the deputy drawled, "but he's the onhappiest man I ever saw."

Miss Crandall did all the talking, and J.B. only nodded in agreement now and then. Shortly after the deputy left, the tall cowboy, Joel, came in. He said he was staying in town because he had been fired the day before by John Buetel, and he volunteered to find the two horses ridden into town by J.B. and Miss Crandall and see that they were fed.

And shortly after that, Sheriff White finished writing, threw his pencil down, and flexed his fingers for the twentieth time. "I always did say writin' is the hardest work there is."

The early-morning sun was warm on their backs as they walked down the boardwalk to Winters' Restaurant. Her arm was looped through his. J.B. still limped on his sore foot. Bits and pieces of their story were being circulated around town, and people stared, clucked, and even smiled at them. All this embarrassed the cowboy, and he kept his head down, letting the broad brim of his hat partially hide his face.

They took a table in a far corner of the restaurant, and pretty, dark-haired, dark-eyed Margaret hurried over, wearing a worry frown. "I heard about it, Miss Crandall. It must have been just terrible. How on earth did you stand it?"

"It's over, Margaret. We won. J.B. and I. We'll get the ranch back now."

The worry frown left. "I'm so happy for you, Miss Crandall."

"Thank you. And by the way, I hope you'll come to the ranch in a few days so you and I can decide how to fix up the foreman's house for you and Joel. He's going to be the new foreman, you know."

The girl's face broke into a wide smile. "That will be fun, Miss Crandall."

"Shine. Since you and I will be seeing a lot of each other, please call me Shine. We'll be the only women on the CC ranch. I have an idea for some curtains, and maybe a rug for the main room, and you'll have some ideas too. It's going to be fun."

Suddenly, for the first time since J.B. had met her, Shine Crandall was all woman. She was talking about womanly things. And she was enjoying it. Could it be she took a man's place only when she had to? Somehow, that pleased J.B. But it saddened him too. It was just going to make what he had to do more difficult.

They ate, J.B. taking on a double order of everything. When they finished, he ordered two ham sandwiches to go. This brought a question to the face of Miss Crandall, but she didn't ask it.

Then came the time that J.B. had been dreading, the time he had been worrying about for the past two hours.

He left the restaurant and limped to the livery barn with her beside him. She studied his face, saw determination, and knew better than to ask questions. He retrieved the blue-roan, then remembered he still didn't have money to pay for the horse's feed.

"It's on me," the stableman said, holding out his right hand. "I heard about what happened. Just let me shake your hand, will you?'

He threw the saddle on the horse's back, cinched it, then turned to face her, trying to think of the proper words. She saved him that chore.

"You don't have to tell me, J.B.," she said solemnly. "You don't even have to tell me why. It's because I'm headstrong. I'm bossy too. And you're an independent cuss who won't be dominated by a woman. Isn't that it?"

He nodded.

"Together we can do anything, J.B. I'll make you a full partner."

He spoke solemnly too. "It would always be your ranch."

She nodded to let him know she understood and touched his arm. "Would you mind, J.B., if I never forget you?"

"No."

"And would you do one more thing for me?" She reached into the pocket of her denim pants, stepped close, and kissed him on the mouth. When their lips met, she slipped a half dozen gold coins into his shirt pocket. "Will you take these?'

The kiss left him with rubbery knees, but he managed to say, "No, I cain't.'

"J.B." Her voice was threatening.

He fumbled the coins out of his pocket, kept one, and handed the rest back to her. "One's enough." He forced a small threat into his own voice. "Take 'em, Shine."

"What will you do if I refuse?" That half smile was pulling at the corners of her mouth again.

He had to grin at her. "Turn you over my knee and spank you."

"You and whose army?" But she allowed him to take her hand and place the coins in it.

That done, he stepped into the saddle. "Where are you heading, J.B.?"

"North. To Colorado. I've always wondered what that country is like."

"Good-bye, J.B."

He reined the blue-roan around and rode at a trot out of town. When he got to the top of the hill on the west side, he had a terrible urge to stop and look back. But he knew that if he did, he would change his mind. He knew he was leaving behind a girl he would never forget and an opportunity that he would never have again.

He muttered to himself, trying to justify his decision. "If there's one thing I cain't stand it's a bossy woman. But," he added painfully, "why does she have to be so sweet and kind and gentle and loyal? And good-natured? And good-lookin'?"

He rode on, stiffly, looking straight ahead. "There ain't one chance in a thousand of a man like me gettin' a girl like that. Not one chance in a million."

Angry with himself now, he talked on. "The smart thing to do is go back. A man has to belong somewhere. But whoever said ol' J.B. Watts was smart."

Suddenly he lifted the reins and brought the blue-roan to a standstill. "Well, maybe it's time ol' J.B. got smart." He turned the horse around. "Come on, Ol' Amigo."

She was walking in a slow, foot-dragging walk back to the hotel. Her hands were deep in the pockets of her Levi's and her head was down. She didn't hear the clip, clop of a horse's hooves come up behind her on the street. She paid no attention when the horse slowed to a walk beside her. It wasn't until her name was called softly that she looked up.

J.B. stopped the horse, leaned forward with his forearms resting on the saddle horn, and looked down at her. "Did you mean it, Shine, about being partners?"

When she looked up, she was pleased and puzzled at the same time. She answered without hesitation, "Yes, J.B."

"In everything?"

The half-smile that he had become familiar with tugged at her mouth. "In everything."

"Would you shake on it?"

The smile widened. "You get off that horse, cowboy, and I'll do better than that."

"Right here in the street?"

"Right here in the street."

Townspeople stared and shook their heads as the young cowboy and the girl stood in the street and sealed the partnership.

THE END

Be sure to check out the next novel in
Doyle Trent's wild west series:

SQUAW MOUNTAIN MASSACRE

LOOKING FOR ACTION & ADVENTURE
AUTHOR ALAN CAILLOU
DELIVERS !

DON'T MISS ANY OF MICHAEL KASNER'S HARD HITTING MILITARY NOVEL SERIES

BLACK OPS

Formed by an elite cadre of government officials, the Black OPS team goes where the law can't - to seek retribution for acts of terror directed against Americans anywhere in the world.

3 BOOK SERIES

Armed with all the tactical advantages of modern technology, battle hard and ready when the free world is threatened - the Peacekeepers are the baddest grunts on the planet.

4 BOOK SERIES

CHOPPER COPS

America is being torn apart as criminal cartels terrorize our cities, dealing drugs and death wholesale. Local police are outgunned, so the President unleashes the U.S. TACTICAL POLICE FORCE. An elite army of super cops with ammo to burn, they swoop down on the hot spots in sleek high-tech attack choppers to win the dirty war and take back America!

4 BOOK SERIES

FROM CALIBER BOOKS

www.calibercomics.com

CALIBER BOOKS

DON'T MISS ANY OF NEIL HUNTER'S NOVELS FROM CALIBER BOOKS

Reporter Les Mason is completing an expose on the Long Point Nuclear Plant. But before he can finish he dies an agonizing death. The doctors are baffled—and there are similar cases to follow...Chris Lane, his girlfriend, and organizer of the Long Point Protestors, discovers Mason's notes, and decides to find out for herself what the plant has to hide.

2 BOOK SERIES

In middle of the 21st century America – over-populated decaying cities are ruled by hi-tech gangs pushing every vice and wastelands are controlled by bands of mutants. Ordinary citizens are oppressed and face a hopeless future. But Marshal T.J. Cade is a new breed of law enforcer. Teamed with his cyborg partner, Janek, Cade takes on these criminals and works in the gray areas of the law to get the job done.

3 BOOK SERIES

The village of Shepthorne England wasn't being gripped, but strangled by a winter's blanket of heavy snow and Arctic temperatures. The trouble began innocently enough with a massive pile-up of autos on frozen roads leading to and from the village. Then, from the sky, a military transport plane with its top secret cargo of devastation crashed down towards the center of the village. Hell was just beginning to touch Shepthorne and its unsuspecting citizens...

FROM CALIBER BOOKS

CALIBER BOOKS

www.calibercomics.com

CALIBER COMICS GOES TO WAR!
HISTORICAL AND MILITARY THEMED GRAPHIC NOVELS

**WORLD WAR ONE:
MO MAN'S LAND**

ISBN: 9781635298123

A look at World War 1 from the French trenches as they faced the Imperial German Army.

CORTEZ AND THE FALL OF THE AZTECS

ISBN: 9781635299779

Cortez battles the Aztecs while in search of Inca gold.

**TROY:
AN EMPIRE UNDER SIEGE**

ISBN: 9781635298635

Homer's famous The Iliad and the Trojan War is given a unique human perspective rather than from the God's.

WITNESS TO WAR

ISBN: 9781635299700

WW2's Battle of the Bulge is seen up close by an embedded female war reporter.

THE LINCOLN BRIGADE

ISBN: 9781635298222

American volunteers head to Spain in the 1930s to fight in their civil war against the fascist regime.

**EL CID:
THE CONQUEROR**

ISBN: 9780982654996

Europe's greatest warrior attempts to unify Spain against invading foreign and domestic armies.

WINTER WAR

ISBN: 9780985749392

At the outbreak of WW2 Finland fights against an invading Soviet army.

**ZULUNATION:
END OF EMPIRE**

ISBN: 9780941613415

The global British Empire and far-reaching influence is threatened by a Zulu uprising in southern Africa.

AIR WARRIORS: WORLD WAR ONE #V1 - V4   *Take to the skies of WW1 as various fighter aces tell their harrowing stories.*
ISBN: 9781635297973 (V1), 9781635297980 (V2), 9781635297997 (V3), 9781635298000 (V4)